Out of the Wilderness

Out of the Wilderness

A Western Quest Series Novel

Stephen L. Turner

SUNSTONE
PRESS

SANTA FE

Sunstone books may be purchased for educational, business, or sales pro-
motional use. For information please write: Special Markets Department,
Sunstone Press,
P.O. Box 2321, Santa Fe, New Mexico 87504-2321.

Book design » Vicki Ahl
Body typeface » Book Antiqua
Printed on acid free paper

Library of Congress Cataloging-in-Publication Data

Turner, Stephen L., 1957-
  Out of the wilderness : a western quest series novel / by Stephen L. Turner.
    p. cm.
  ISBN 978-0-86534-709-0 (pbk. : alk. paper)
  1. Scots-Irish--South Carolina--Fiction. 2. South Carolina--History--Colonial
period, ca. 1600-1775--Fiction. I. Title.
  PS3620.U76596O98 2009
  813'.6--dc22

                        2008053554

Published in

WWW.SUNSTONEPRESS.COM
SUNSTONE PRESS / POST OFFICE BOX 2321 / SANTA FE, NM 87504-2321 /USA
(505) 988-4418 / ORDERS ONLY (800) 243-5644 / FAX (505) 988-1025

Foreword

THIS BOOK IS A WORK OF fiction based on the few facts that are known about Thomas Turner of Ireland, my great-great-great-great-grandfather. An effort has been made to use historically correct names, dates, locations, and events when they are known. Glimpses of Thomas Turner are seen on deeds, maps, and early documents of colonial South Carolina. The location of the plantation is known from the deed and early maps of Marlboro County. This novel is written from his viewpoint as a fictionalized account of what his life must have been like in the remote parts of the forested wilderness of colonial America. Marlboro County was a very isolated and thinly populated area before the Revolutionary War. It was mostly continuous mixed hardwood and pine forest interrupted by streams and rare homesteads. We know that Thomas Turner came to this wilderness area, carved out a plantation and raised a family. From pension records, we know that the Turners fought in the Revolutionary War with the American patriots. I hope this will give the reader a glimpse into his life.

Acknowledgment

THANKS ARE DUE TO ED S. and Bill Turner of Tularosa, New Mexico, who did much of the original research. Thanks are also due to Buzz Watson of Sierra Vista, Arizona, who organized it into a readily usable CD, and to Ella Bullard of Baird, Texas, who is a veritable fountain of family history. Special thanks are due to Larenda Roberts for her patient work as editor and my father, Aaron Lynn Turner, for proof reading.

~BANSHEE~
Belfast

1

THE FOG LAY HEAVY ON
Lough Belfast in the moments before a chilly dawn
March 15, 1749. Water fell in fat cold drops from
the furled sails and rigging onto the oak deck of
the topsail schooner *Banshee*. Her spars and timbers
creaked and groaned quietly as if in anticipation of
the long trip ahead. The slowly rising tide pulled
gently at her moorings.

I had sailed on her many times, but this time
was different. Never before had I felt the weight of
responsibility rest so heavily on my seventeen year
old shoulders. The muscles in my neck and shoulders
tensed, and my stomach was tied in knots; never
before had so much been expected of me. I had much
to prove to my father and brothers, and much to
prove to myself. For all the world to see, I was calm
and confident. I was not about to let anyone know
otherwise.

My task was not so large. I was to travel halfway around the world, to a place I had never been, buy land I had never seen, and become a successful planter. The closest I had come to being a farmer was to collect rent on some of my father's farms near Belfast. I was to carve a successful, profitable plantation out of the Carolina wilderness. I might as well try to move a mountain one stone at a time. I felt overwhelmed and unprepared, but I dared not show it. I was the seventh son, the favorite, and Father had great confidence that I was up to the challenge.

My thoughts drifted back to the sequence of events that had transpired to bring me to this pivotal point. In 1690, after another failed rebellion by the Irish Catholics in the north of Ireland, King William had resolved to expand upon what King James I had begun in 1607. He confiscated the lands of the rebellious Irish lords and divided their great estates out to loyal subjects. Previously, only Anglicans had been allowed. But to check them from becoming too powerful in their new enclave, he had seen fit to give land to dissenter families like ours: Puritans, Presbyterians, Methodists and Quakers. Our family had been more than willing to leave the famine that had struck the Scottish lowlands that year. King William had sought to pacify the Ulster region once and for all. The Irish nobles had been exiled or executed, but the common Catholic Irishmen had remained as crofters and craftsmen. Someone had to provide the labor, for there were not enough transplanted settlers to do all the work. So the Irish had been left there to suffer at the hands of the usurping English lords and to sow the seeds of discord for many years to come. The Irish had risen in numerous bloody small revolts killing hundreds of Protestant "invaders." But for now, we had an unspoken truce.

Being Presbyterians, we were distrusted by the Anglicans as well as the Catholics. The other dissenters found themselves in the same situation. Like us, they were seen as less than desirable by the good English Anglicans. I hoped that in the Carolinas I would be judged for my character and not my creed.

Since the time of my great-grandfather's arrival in Ireland, our family had gradually come to prosper. My parents, Josiah and Mary, had seven sons and three daughters. They had acquired several good farms, and had developed a profitable merchant and trading enterprise. What my great-grandfather had begun with one leaky coastal lugger had grown into a small fleet of trading vessels. There were a dozen coastal traders and three topsail schooners. There were offices and warehouses in Belfast, Kingston, Jamaica, and Charleston, South Carolina.

The jewel of the trading fleet was the *Banshee*. She was 120 feet from stem to stern, thirty-five feet across the beam, with sleek beautiful lines. She was built of the best seasoned oak, fitted with the finest canvas sails, the best Manila rigging and Stockholm tar. Below the waterline, copper sheathing kept out the boring toredo worms, and slowed the growth of speed-robbing seaweed. She was armed with four six-pound cannons to a side, and two more in the stern. She also carried six one-pound swivel guns.

The footsteps of the approaching crew interrupted my thoughts and returned me to my present duties. I was master of the *Banshee*, the owner's representative on board and responsible for the ship and her cargo. The sailing master, Brian Clancy, answered only to me. He was responsible for handling the ship and her crew.

Brian knew his business. The crew respected him, as I did, too. He was a raw-boned, red-headed, blue-eyed Irish Catholic, with a weathered face and a voice like a bull.

"It has the looks of a fine mornin', Thomas!"

"Aye, Brian! Are the lads ready to go?"

The rest of the crew was lined up on the dock, handing their sea chests and bags on to the *Banshee*. They were a good group of men who could be trusted in a gale. My father paid all of them a standard sailor's wage depending on their job description and experience, but he also distributed a percentage of the profits from the voyage to the crew. They all had an interest in the success of each trip.

Patrick McNamara, the first mate, was keeping order on deck. He was from County Cork of a Catholic father and a Protestant serving girl. He was unclaimed and lacking respect on land, but fully accepted for his obvious ability at sea.

Banshee's carpenter, Charles Moore, was an English Methodist. With the proper tools and wood he could build anything. His carpenter's mate, Keenan Harman, was a young apprentice of only 14 who showed promise in his skills. Between voyages he worked with both a cooper and a wheelwright. He could already make barrels that didn't leak and repair broken wheels.

Our boson was a taut Dutch sailor named Jan Van Pelt. He was responsible for the complicated rigging of the ship. There was none better in a ship this size.

Conner McLean was our gunner and smith. If it was metal, he could make it or repair it. He was a Scot with a quick wit and ready smile. He could lay a six-pound cannon with an eagle's eye. He trained all hands on the cannons when we were at sea. He kept the guns ready, the muskets oiled, and the cutlasses sharpened. His gunner's mate, Sean Perkins, was a slender Irish orphan of fifteen. He had worked for a blacksmith before joining the ship.

Our cook was a mixed race Jamaican known only as "John Cook." The details of his real name and past were overlooked because of his ability in the galley and his skills with healing herbs. His mate was a skinny twelve year old, Zachary Hawkins. The ship's boy who waited tables and did odd chores was an Irish Catholic boy of ten, Dylan Caswell. Both boys' fathers were tenants on my father's farms. They were fast friends who became the mascots of the ship's crew.

The ship was named *Banshee* for the mythical Celtic female spirit who came screaming with the wind and darkness to steal men's souls. And the topsail schooner *Banshee* had fabled speed and nimble handling. She was the envy of many a ship's master.

"Thomas, the lading was finished yesterday. All the goods and stores are aboard." McNamara had read my mind.

"Aye. Thank ye, Patrick. Mr. Clancy, Patrick here tells me the cargo is secure. We may sail when you see fit."

"All hands to unmoor ship," Clancy roared.

Van Pelt directed the loosening and storage of the cables that held *Banshee* to the dock.

"Van Pelt, you great ox of a Dutchman, has the tide begun to ebb?"

"Aye, aye, Mr. Clancy."

"Then get those sons of farmers to set the jib sail and bring her head around!"

As the jib sail filled, it slowly turned the bow away from the dock and pointed north into Lough Belfast. Just as the first rays of sunlight appeared on the port side, Clancy ordered the mainsail set. The blocks creaked and groaned as the crojack yard was hoisted, setting the large fore-and-aft sail. The large boom of the mainsail was allowed to swing to starboard until it billowed full with the dawn breeze.

"McNamara, hold her steady north northeast."

"Van Pelt, set the foresail!"

The sail was set and the boom swung starboard until it, too, was drawing tight.

"Thomas, I believe the lads have gotten fat and lazy while they have been ashore!"

"The shepherd's pie and ale have made them slow, Brian! The wind and sea will soon set them right again."

"Now if it would not be imposing on yourself Jan, would ye kindly set the main topsail?!"

Under Van Pelt's watchful gaze, four of the hands climbed up the main rat-lines and untied the canvas reef-points that kept the sail against the spar. As the topsail dropped, it filled with the breeze. The men on the deck hauled on the lines until it was drawing tight and secured.

No sooner were the four back on the deck, than Clancy ordered the fore topsail set. Other hands ran up the rat-lines and dropped the fore topsail. As the clew lines pulled the sail to catch the wind, the added force of the topsails caused a surge in speed. Foam creamed along *Banshee's* bow and the deck tilted gently away from the wind.

"Keep it thus, McNamara!"

The fog lifted as we sailed north over Lough Belfast, and the glory of the March sunrise broke across the sky. The wind continued from the west as we reached the open sea. We made an easy run to the east before coming about on a southerly course down the Irish Sea.

By early afternoon, the fabled Isle of Man was under our lee. I called Zachary and Dylan to me.

"Look boys! The Isle of Man. It was the most sacred place to the ancient Druids."

"Who were the Druids, sir?" Dylan asked.

"Now, Dylan, as an Irishman you should be knowing that they were the holy men, priests, and healers of the "Old Ones," the Britons, Erse and Gaels. The Romans feared their power over the people. They came here, to this island, to destroy them. They killed every man, woman and child they found. They burned their buildings, and even killed all their animals. It is said some of the Druids escaped and lived hiding in the wild places of England, Scotland, Wales, and Ireland."

"Are there any of them left alive now, sir?" Zachary asked.

"Aye. I believe their children's children live among us where the old ways are still known. They had a sea god called Ler who could take the form of a dolphin. Some sailors believe it is Ler who watches over seamen, so will never harm a dolphin."

"I saw a sailor with a dolphin tattooed on his arm in Belfast," Dylan added.

"Aye, and I saw one with a naked lady!" Zachary laughed.

Clancy had the topsails taken in and double reefs in the fore and main sails as dusk approached.

"There's too many drunk Englishmen about in these waters to go a'sailin' like blazes into the night!"

The *Banshee*'s speed dropped to no more than three knots as the way came off of her. Clancy set the men at their watch stations in the bow and the foretopmast tree to watch for trouble.

After a good supper, I reviewed our bill of lading with McNamara.

"Now, Patrick, I see we have ballast of iron and lead bars. Those will bring good money in the colonies. Linen, cotton and woolen goods in barrels. Good Indian and Ceylon tea; is it shipped high, Patrick?"

"Are you taking me for a farmer, Mr. Thomas? Of course it is!"

"Kegs of nails, boxes of house wares. Coffee beans in barrels. Do you ever drink the stuff, Patrick?"

"It is too dear for a poor sailorman. A dish of tea and a tot of whisky are more to m' taste."

"Aye. I like the tea myself. The coffee is too bitter. I don't care for the wicked brew you call whisky. It's but poor Irish poteen cooked over a peat fire; 'tis made to poison a good Presbyterian like me."

We laughed and continued the list.

"Boxes of hand tools, plows, and farmers' goods."

"An' we'll trade it for sugar and rum in the islands, rice and tobacco at Charleston, like always, sir. The poor sailormen will finally have two coins to rub together!"

"And you'll spend yours on ale and wicked women as usual!"

To avoid the rock-bound coast of France, we stood as far to the west as we could across the Bay of Biscay. Here the sea was rougher, but *Banshee* shouldered through the waves like a racehorse. We had a full cargo hold and plenty of supplies, so there was no need to stop at Corunna or Lisbon. We set our course for the Azores where we would replenish our water and stores.

About a day's sail short of the Azores, the mainmast look out hailed the deck.

"Strange sail to the southwest. Two of 'em there are. Look to be lateen rigged, sir."

Mr. Clancy raced up the rat-lines with his telescope to settle next to the look-out.

"Where away, lad? Ah, I see 'em. Keep your eyes open, and sing out!"

"All hands, all hands to make sail!"

When he reached the deck the crew was puzzled, but ready for orders.

"Men, there is a nasty pair of Moorish dogs tryin' to catch our tail. Let's show 'em a clean set of heels!"

"Patrick, hold 'er steady for St. Michaels. Van Pelt, set all the sail she'll bear."

The fore and mainsails were already set and drawing, as were both topsails and the jib. He had the men set the upper and lower staysails and the fore topmast staysail.

"Zachary, Dylan, you lads toss the log."

As the line spun off the reel, Dylan held the 28 second sandglass. When the last grain had fallen he yelled, "Nip!"

Zachary read the colored strings woven into the line and reported to Mr. Clancy. "Fourteen knots, sir! We're flying!"

As he spoke, the weather-cock at the helm began to flutter. The wind which had been steady from the northeast all morning shifted to east northeast. The sails were brought around further to maintain the same course, but it cost us some speed. The next cast of the log showed our speed had dropped to twelve knots. But the shift of wind brought the two Barbary pirates closer to us, and it appeared they would intercept us within an hour. The look-out reported they both carried one large gun in the bows, but none along the sides. Their decks were crowded with men, maybe fifty or so each.

The look-out called down in horror, "Sir! Another sail due west! One ship, lateen rigged, heading southeast!"

Clancy and I had a hurried meeting by the wheel.

"Thomas, we can't get away from them. They have our escape blocked to the west, south and east. The wind is foul for a run to the north. We could take a chance and try to run by the ship to the west, but his friends will soon be in range to fire at our stern."

"What do you propose, Brian?"

"Tom, if we let them get close enough to board us we're dead men. There are too many of them in even one ship to overpower us. Their ship's sides are unprotected. Our best chance is to use our greater advantage in fire-power to keep them away. I want to bear down on the two to the east, loaded with chain shot to disable their sails and rigging. With a little luck, they'll never get close to us."

"Aye, I agree. And what of their friend to the west?"

"We change course and bear down on him and shoot his sails away, too."

"Three against one?"

"We're Irishmen, Tom. We're used to long odds."

I laughed to myself, and thought "and used to losing, too."

"Van Pelt, get the topsails in quick!"

"Conner, load all the six-pounders with chain shot. Load the swivels with canister. Run out port, starboard and stern guns!"

"Sean, open the arms chest. Get every man two loaded muskets, two pistols, and a boarding pike!"

"Mr. Moore, get the boarding netting in place, and prepare to repel boarders!"

"John Cook, douse the galley fires, and report on deck to help load the guns and muskets!"

"Zachary and Dylan, help Sean loading the muskets and pistols, and don't shoot yourselves in the foot!"

"Patrick, lay a course to run parallel to these Moorish dogs to the east!"

Banshee looked as if someone had kicked over an anthill. The topsails were furled and all the guns and small arms loaded. We had closed the distance to the nearest pirate to within fifty yards. Conner reported all cannons and swivels loaded and manned on the port side. With a nod from Mr. Clancy, Conner ordered "Aim for the rigging and sails. Swivels sweep the decks!"

The gun captains carefully laid their guns, with smoldering slow-match in their hands.

"On the up roll, on my order: Fire!"

All four port guns fired chain shot with whirling, wicked accuracy. Ropes parted. The two huge sails were shredded to rags. The way quickly came off the first ship. The swivels had slain a dozen men, and blood was running in the scuppers.

We reached the second ship which popped away at us with muskets. Once we were ahead of the second ship, but before she could fire her bow gun, we fired both stern guns. We put the helm over to rake them with our starboard guns. We destroyed their sails. The swivels left bloody gaps on her decks. Both ships were left in complete disarray.

"Patrick, make for our friend to the west! Van Pelt, set her topsails again!"

Banshee lurched as she swung hard to port. The sails were soon drawing with the wind across our stern. The guns were reloaded and run out again. Like her namesake, *Banshee* descended on her foe like a fiend from hell. Our attack was totally unexpected. Their bow chaser fired one hurried shot, missing us by 200 feet.

As we closed to within fifty yards, our port guns opened fire. *Banshee* surged past the wounded predator. As we wore ship, we fired our stern chasers, then our starboard guns. Both sails had collapsed in a confused tangle on the deck, covering the carnage wrought by the swivels. As she lay dead in the water, we steered across her stern.

"Van Pelt, spill our wind. McLean, reload the starboard guns with solid shot, and reload the swivels with canister."

The *Banshee* came gliding by the stern with just enough speed to maintain steerage way. Moors began appearing over the gunwales with muskets.

"Do ye strike, ye sons of evil?! Strike or I'll sink you now!"

They responded with musket fire. We had expected such an answer and had taken cover.

"Conner, aim just below the waterline on the down roll. Swivels, sweep the garbage from their decks. Fire!"

All port cannons fired in unison. The transom of the pirate collapsed into rubble. She began to sink rapidly. The swivel guns had quieted the muskets. The Moors launched one boat as we set sail back to the east. As we watched, the wretched vessel disappeared below the surface.

"Patrick, lay us along side those two cripples!"

We decreased sail as we drew across the stern of the nearest. She had made some effort at repairs, but still could not sail.

"Do ye strike, or do we sink your heathen souls?"

With curses and shaking fists, they replied with musket fire. The starboard guns put paid on the debt we owed them. The ship began to slowly settle into the sea. The swivels had done their job well, as no boat or survivors appeared from the wreckage. The final ship had managed to jury-rig a sail from the fore mast. She was attempting to use the wind to aim her one great bow gun at us. We turned from their line of fire.

Suddenly, a lone white man climbed from the wreckage and dived from the stern. He swam desperately towards us. As he drew nearer, we could see he was no Moor. The pirates began to fire at him. Our swivels barked out, killing ten or twelve men on her stern. The swimmer cried out: "Help me! I'm English! Help me!"

We threw him a line, hoisting him aboard. He was exhausted and shaking from his escape. He had been wounded in the right elbow by a musket ball. Conner had anticipated the next orders and had reloaded the guns with solid shot. On Clancy's order all four fired into her transom. She began to sink quickly by the stern. A solitary boat put off from the sinking ship with six men rowing for their lives.

"Sir?" McLean said.

"Let them alone unless they fire on us. Two days rowing a boat may make honest men of them!"

We all laughed and sensed a great feeling of relief. We had taken on three Barbary pirates, and emerged unscathed. From a nearly helpless situation, we had not just escaped, but proven victorious.

"Patrick, set our course for St. Michaels. Conner, clear from action. Van Pelt, set all the sail she'll carry. Mr. Cook, what are ye doing standing there like a moon calf? Get below and fix a fine hot meal for these good men! Thomas, as we saved the cargo from those thievin' pirates, would the company be willin' to share out a wee dram of our good Irish whisky for the lads?"

"Aye. Zachary, fetch out a few bottles of our best whisky for the hands. None of Mr. Clancy's bust-head poison, if ye please."

2

OUR NEW FRIEND PROVED to be a young Englishman, Mark Cunningham. He was a lanky sixteen year old. He had been a passenger on a packet brig that had been attacked by the same three ships. They had boarded the brig and brutally killed most of her crew and passengers, including Mark's father. They had sent the captured brig back to Morocco with a prize crew. The survivors were to be sold as slaves. Mark had jumped into the sea in a futile effort to escape, but was pulled from the sea by one of the pirate ships. As the brig had already sailed, they planned to send him in with their next group of prisoners. During the chaos created by our unexpected aggressive response, he had managed to free himself. His father had been a botanist on his way to India to manage an indigo plantation for the East India Company. Mark was his apprentice. His mother and siblings had died of fever the previous year.

We had John Cook splint his arm. He said the wound was clean and had made a clean break just above the elbow. He had dressed the wound with an herbal poultice.

"Mark, we will put you ashore in St. Michaels with money for passage back to England. If you would like, you may join our crew. I think you could be a great help to us in the colonies. We'll pay a fair wage, plus a bonus if we make a profit."

A look of sadness clouded his face. "Sir, I have no family other than some distant cousins. I'll throw my lot in with you."

We soon reached St. Michaels, the main port in the Azores. *Banshee* dropped anchor in the harbor, and Mr. Clancy granted the men shore leave. McNamara was responsible for arranging for the water hoy to refill our casks, and John Cook was to buy our fresh stores of vegetables, fruit, meat and bread. We would eat well the next few days!

Most of the crew kicked up "Bob's your uncle" in St. Michaels. I took a tour of the countryside by donkey. It wasn't a very dignified way to travel, but it sure beat walking. There were lots of pretty small farms, orchards and vineyards.

After a night ashore, all hands were present to set sail. We hoped to pick up the southeast trade winds somewhere south of the Azores. For now, the winds came from the east, so we angled away to the southwest. On the third day, the wind began to veer a little to the south, and by the fourth day we were fully in the true trades.

Clancy and McNamara plotted our course to touch at Barbados, then run up to Jamaica. Once the course was set, hardly a sail was touched for ten days when the forbidding eastern shore of Barbados was in view. We hauled our wind and altered course for Bridgetown on the southwest corner of the island. We replenished our fresh water and stores. The next morning we set sail for Jamaica. I was anxious to be away to reach the Carolinas.

We steered straight northwest for Jamaica. In four days we were in sight of Kingston. We picked up a harbor pilot to guide us through the treacherous shoals and reefs at the harbor mouth. We passed the ruins of Port Royal to the starboard. A great earthquake and storm had submerged most of it, but Kingston was a sight to behold! Ships of every nation and description filled the harbor. A British 64 gun warship dominated the anchorage, plus a 34 gun frigate and a sloop of war. There were merchant ships of every flag from coastal traders to East Indiamen. Ships' boats skimmed over the surface of the harbor like insects on errands known only to them.

A boat came out from the harbormaster's office to show us where to anchor until we were ready to dock for off-loading our cargo. I was rowed ashore to visit our company shipping office. I took Mark with me to see a good surgeon I knew who could evaluate his elbow.

The surgeon didn't think any other treatment was necessary, and complimented the care John Cook had provided. He told Mark to keep it in a sling a few more weeks. I paid him a half-crown and gave Mark ten Spanish dollars to buy the things he needed that had been lost to the pirates. I gave him directions to find the shipping office. The sign would read "Turner Shipping and Trade, Josiah Turner and Sons."

On the way there, I spied my brother William walking along the wharf.

"William! William Turner, ahoy!"

"Thomas? Well met, little brother! How is the blessed

seventh son? What news of home?"

We walked on to the company offices and shared news of home and markets. I introduced him to Mark when he arrived. William was fascinated by the story of our encounter with the Barbary pirates.

"Are ye mad, brother? Could the swift *Banshee* not outrun them?"

"No, brother. They had us trapped from the east, west and south. The wind was foul for an escape to the north."

"But why did you endanger the cargo? After ye crippled the devils, ye went back to sink them!"

"Would you have them raid us again after they repaired their sails? The next time, we might not be so fortunate. Would you only chase a wolf away from the sheep when you could kill it? Nay, brother!"

"I suppose you are in the right of it. Thank God we lost none of the men, and even gained a new friend."

"Mark here is to be my clerk. Can you write left-handed?"

"I am right-handed, but if I do not hurry too much, I believe I can write legibly enough."

"William, we are ready to unload our Jamaica cargo. What do ye have for us to take to the colonies?"

"Rum in casks and cases of bottles, and good Jamaican sugar in barrels."

"Have ye heard of our true mission?"

"Aye. I had a letter from Father. On the Pee Dee River in South Carolina, isn't it?"

"So I have been told. I have never seen it, but brother James has it selected. I am anxious to get there."

The next morning, the *Banshee* ghosted along at a snail's

pace to the company wharf. Our goods for Jamaica were off-loaded and the cargo for the colonies placed in the hold. The water casks had been filled, and fresh fruit, vegetables and bread put aboard. We missed our tide for a departure that day, but resolved to catch the morning tide. That night, William had a supper prepared for me and Mr. Clancy. Their hired cook did a wonderful job. It was good to see my cousins again. They were growing into beautiful young ladies. Their mother had died two years before of the fever. We did not stay too late, as we had an early morning planned.

At daybreak all the hands were present and sober from their run ashore. Our office there had paid them their wages. Some had enjoyed spending it, while others had the company transfer it to their accounts in Belfast for their families. With only the main topsail and jib set, the pilot guided us safely out of Kingston harbor. A small pilot boat was towed behind for his return. Mr. Clancy had the topsail struck, and both the fore and mainsails set, but double reefed to reduce our speed as we carefully sailed along the coast of Jamaica eastward to the Santo Domingo Channel. There we turned northeast under modest sail.

We were just through the channel at sunset. Mr. Clancy had *Banshee* anchor for the night rather than risk striking an unseen reef or shoal in the infamous Bahamas Passage ahead of us. We dropped anchor in twenty fathom water with good holding in hard sand. Some of the men set about dropping fishing lines over the side. Soon, they had enough fish to feed the whole crew. John Cook rolled the cleaned fish in a spicy mixture of cornmeal and flour and fried it. It was served with fresh vegetables, cornmeal and fresh Jamaican beer. It was a feast for all of us.

At daybreak, we hoisted the anchor and set limited sails to thread our way through the Bahamas Passage. Logan Perkins, fourteen, the younger brother of Sean, was in the bow with a lead line continuously testing the depth of the water. An experienced hand was stationed in the foretop to watch for shoals and reefs. In the clear water, they could be distinguished by changes in water color. The water became a paler blue as it got more shallow, and green where it was very shallow. We eased along at just about four knots. Another lookout was posted in the maintop to watch for strange sails, as this area was notorious for pirates. We reached Nassau by late afternoon, and anchored there. The men were given shore liberty for the night.

Dawn found us raising anchor from Nassau's lovely harbor. We were bound to finish the last leg of the Bahamas Passage that day. From there it would be clear sailing to the American coast. Once clear of the passage, we were anxious to pick up the pace.

"Van Pelt!" Clancy roared, "shake out the reefs in the mainsails and set the topsails!"

Banshee responded like a racehorse to a whip. As the sails filled, we gently heeled to leeward and she rushed through the deep water throwing a fine bow wave. Once we were in the northward course of the Gulf Stream we were speeding over the waves. We dropped anchor in Savannah that night, as it was too late to try to negotiate the notorious sand bars and shoals that paralleled the American coast in that area. The next day, we stood out far enough to avoid them. Soon, the channel markers for Charleston were sighted, and we cautiously threaded our way into the spacious harbor.

Charleston was indeed a beautiful harbor. The harbor master's boat guided us to our berth at the company dock. With only the jib and reefed main topsail drawing, we just had steerage way to slowly weave through the busy harbor. We moored at the dock just across from the company sign. A booming voice echoed from an open second story window.

"Welcome, Thomas! We've been expecting ye!"

"Dear brother James! It is good to see ye. Are Lucy and the children well?"

"Aye, brother. Let me come down and we'll talk a spell."

James was the eldest of my brothers, twelve years my senior. He was a handsome man with thick red hair, blue eyes and over six feet tall. He had already left home to work in Charleston by the time I was in long-breeches.

"Thomas, I have found some beautiful land up the Great Pee Dee River. I can't wait to show it to you. It is about a half-day's ride northeast of Cheraw Landing where Phill's Creek crosses the new road."

"Have you now, brother? Is it not a pile of rocks in a peat bog?"

"No, youngster. It is four hundred eighty-three acres of prime land, well forested, with rich deep soil. If you approve, we'll complete the purchase from the widow, Mrs. Quick. Her other land joins it, and she is eager to sell it."

"What crops are grown on it? Does it have a great house with white columns and twenty servants?"

"Baby brother, you know I would not deny you the opportunity to develop it to suit yourself! There isn't any cropland yet, nor a house, barn or servants!"

I had envisioned cleared land, plowed fields, a house, barns, and fenced pastures for the livestock. This was going to be a much bigger job than I had imagined.

"Thomas, we are buying it for only one and a half Spanish dollars per acre! The timber on it alone is worth twice that. It has good soils for growing indigo and tobacco. It will take hard work and time, but it will make ye a rich man!"

"Aye. Nothing good comes easy. When do I see this garden of Eden?"

"We have business to tend to here first. We must shift cargo on the *Banshee*. Then we will go to Georgetown, where the Pee Dee meets the sea. It is a fair harbor, and we have established an office there to handle the timber and rice trade. We have several scows there for the river trade. I have a trusted assistant there, a colonial named Paul Johnson. Our brother, Edward, is to take over running the office when he arrives from Ireland."

Edward was the sixth son. We had grown up very close to each other, and had always looked out for one another. I couldn't think of anyone I would rather have close by than Edward.

Most of *Banshee*'s cargo was unloaded, and she was reloaded with barrels of rice and tobacco, and a few precious water-tight kegs of indigo. Ounce for ounce it was more valuable than gold. The ballast of iron and lead was replaced with rock and locally made bricks for the trip back to Belfast.

"Thomas, I'd like to show ye the newest venture we have undertaken here. Come with me to the ship yard."

We walked a short distance when I saw the most unusual ship. She had three masts, with tall, almost sheer sides, and disproportionately long to her beam. She had a gaping wide and long hold, bigger than any I had ever seen. The masts were unusually tall and stout. She was rigged with great heavy cargo tackle fore and aft. She was obviously built to be stable in any kind of weather or sea, but would never touch half the speed of

Banshee. Across her stern her name was carved and painted with gilded paint: *Pride of Charleston*.

"James, what is this monster?"

"She is a ship built specifically to carry timber, spars and masts. The forests here are blest with some of the world's best trees for making masts and spars. We will work them up at our mast yard in Georgetown. The logs can be floated down the Pee Dee to us there from all over the northern part of the state and southern North Carolina. There is a tremendous market for them. What do you think of her?"

"I think she will make money for the company, and makes us all as rich as lords! What will she carry on her return voyages?"

"Oh, just regular trade goods, but a vast amount at any one time. Because of her size and strength, we will arm her with nine pounders, eight to a side, two nine pound stern guns, and eight two pound swivels. Only a foolish pirate would dream of attacking her."

"I'm impressed! Was this your idea?"

"Aye. Father believes there will be an even greater demand if war breaks out with the Dutch, Spanish or French."

"James, she is no swan, but I believe she may be a golden goose!"

The men were given liberty as James and I took passage on one of our beamy coastal traders to Georgetown. I took Keenan, Sean, Logan and Mark with me. We took adequate silver coins with us in a chest marked "pewter house wares." Within a day we were in Widyah Bay, standing in for Georgetown.

Paul Johnson met us at the wharf. The Turner office there was only a clapboard building, as the brick building was still under construction. The warehouses contained countless barrels of rice, tobacco, and indigo, eventually destined for European markets. Georgetown was much smaller than Charleston, and lacked its civilized touch. But it possessed a raw, robust vigor that foretold of prosperity to come.

Paul secured one of the company's scows for our trip up the river. It was wide, sturdy and open decked. There was no hold. The bottom had been planked over to provide a flat bottom. Cargo was secured on the deck. It was an ugly slug of a vessel. It had one mast stepped far forward that carried a modest lug sail set high enough to stay out of the way of the deck. There was tackle to use the spar for hoisting cargo into the scow. Along each side were massive oak oars, and a huge steering oar in the pointed stern. The crew appeared to be mostly slaves. It was their job to row the great oars that would propel the scow upstream against the current, and to handle the cargo. A white man held the tiller, and another was in the bow with the lead line. Both were armed with three pistols, a cutlass and long whips.

The scow carried farm implements, tools, a few household items, and iron and lead bars. A small forge and anvil were loaded on board, as were a pair of draft oxen and their fittings. They were so gentle, they hardly protested as they were loaded on board. Also, a good solid horse was loaded. He was a gelding of about fourteen hands and stoutly built. He was obviously not going to win the Irish Derby, but he could work in the fields, pull a wagon, and make a passable saddle horse. Finally, a moderate sized wagon had been disassembled and loaded aboard.

Our trip up the Great Pee Dee was assisted by a slight breeze, which the lug sail was able to capture to our advantage. With the slaves also rowing, we seemed to be making good time.

The lower river was wide and lazy. It was lined with cypress and backed by a huge low-lying forest of swamps. We saw where dikes were being built to systematically flood or drain rice fields. There were rafts of timber heading down the river, bound together by a perimeter of logs chained together and secured with spikes. I could see that a spar yard in Georgetown should do well. Soon we came to a smaller river joining the Pee Dee from the north.

"What is that river, James?"

"That would be the Little Pee Dee. That is why we sometimes call this one the Great Pee Dee to distinguish them. Farther north, the Little Pee Dee is called the Lumber River. Huge amounts of timber come down here to the coast."

Farther up the Pee Dee, a great slow-flowing wide river fanned out to form a swamp of flooded woodland. There was a low island in the swamp where it gently merged with the Pee Dee from the southwest.

"Thomas, this is the Lynches River. It fans out wide and shallow, so it is not navigable. The island you can see from here is called Snow Island, as it is really a salt dome. There is an old salt works and the ruins of a mission there."

The scow's lug sail, through careful adjustments, was able to be used most of the way to Cheraw. The oarsmen did not seem to get tired, but rowed together, chanting to maintain their rhythm. We passed a wide pretty creek James identified as Phill's Creek. A few miles upstream, the creek formed the sloping western boundary of the property we wanted to buy. Soon we reached Cheraw Landing, across the river from the town of Cheraw, perched on a high bluff. We tied up at the dock at the ferry landing. We hired horses from the ferryman's livery stable and traveled along the "new road" towards Brightsville. After several miles we reached the ford where the road crossed Phill's Creek.

"This would be the west corner of your plantation, Thomas. The road marks the north boundary, the creek the west. The fence on Mrs. Quick's land makes the east boundary. The fence of the Irby plantation makes the south boundary. It is four hundred eighty-three acres of prime forest, waiting for the axe and the plow."

"It's beautiful, James. Let's ride the boundaries."

There were tall straight pines, beautiful tupelo trees, huge white oaks, sweet gums and hickory trees. We saw deer, turkey, squirrels and other small game. There was no fence along the creek. We soon reached a stout rail fence marking Jonathan Irby's land. It was mostly forested as far as we could see. Following the fence line, we found that it intersected the Widow Quick's land. Again, it was a stout, well-built fence. We followed it until it emerged on the road. It was a beautiful property.

We arrived at Mrs. Quick's spacious cabin by late afternoon. There were sturdy log barns and outbuildings. It looked like there were forty or more acres in tobacco and indigo, plus smaller fields of corn, oats and wheat. The corn was barely breaking through in rows. The wheat and oats stood thigh high. The indigo was just breaking out new leaves. Field workers were transplanting tobacco plants into the fields. There was a large garden with greens, cabbage and onions. We tied the horses to the porch rail and stepped up onto the porch.

"Well, Mr. Turner. Come in, come in. This must be your brother. Welcome!"

"Hello, Mrs. Quick! Aye, this is my brother, Thomas. These

young men are Mark, Keenan, Sean, and Logan."

"I'm pleased to meet you, Mrs. Quick."

"Ma'am!" the youngsters echoed.

"Would you boys take the horses to the barn? One of the men will put out feed and hay for them. Mr. Turner, won't you and your brother step inside? We have business to discuss."

We stepped into the well-made cabin, comfortably furnished in locally made furniture. We agreed to the terms of $723 milled Spanish dollars to be paid the next day at the closing in Cheraw. We would be allowed immediate possession, including the timber. We agreed to travel to Cheraw together in the morning.

Mrs. Quick provided a fine supper of ham, baked sweet potatoes, greens and corn bread. We bedded down in the barn loft on fragrant hay. The wool blankets she provided were warm. We slept well that night.

The next morning we were treated to a fine breakfast of biscuits, eggs, smoked bacon and tea. The horses were soon saddled. Mrs. Quick would travel in her buggy driven by one of her servants. We returned our horses to the livery and Mrs. Quick left her buggy there under the care of her servant. We took the ferry across to Cheraw. There was a wagon there with rows of seats that for six pence would take us up the steep hill to Cheraw. It dropped us at the Bank of Cheraw.

James produced a letter of credit drawn on our Charleston bank. The Bank of Cheraw had been warned of our need for silver. We would use our own only if absolutely necessary. It was carefully counted out to Mrs. Quick, who in turn counted out $23 and deposited the remaining $700 back into the bank. She signed the deed over to me. Marlboro County, where the land was located, was part of a three county district centered on Cheraw, which also included Chesterfield and Darlington Counties. We walked across the street to the Cheraw District Clerk's office to file our deed. I paid the registration fee of one pound sterling, which was about $2, four bits.

Pounds, Dutch talers and Spanish dollars or pesos were all circulated, but the most common were the Spanish dollars. They were also called pieces eight. They contained one ounce of silver, and had marking on the back making it easy to divide into pie-shaped wedges of eight bits to the dollar. Halves, quarters and eighths were freely circulated and widely accepted.

Our business complete, we bid farewell to Mrs. Quick. We unloaded the wagon, farm implements, iron, lead, oxen and horse. We paid the livery and ferryman, Mr. Llewellyn, to tend our stock, watch over our goods, and assemble the wagon before we returned. Now that the land was bought, we revealed our plans to the others as we made our trip back down the river. I offered each of them a chance to leave the ship and return to work on the plantation. They were to clear a site for building a cabin and farm buildings. Their pay would increase by 50 percent, and they would receive an interest in the profits of the plantation. All of them readily accepted. Mark was to be the plantation bookkeeper and botanist. Keenan would be our carpenter and in charge of building the cabin. Sean was to be the smith, and help with other farm work. Logan would be our jack of all trades to help where he was needed.

Logan and Sean agreed, but asked a favor. They requested that I retrieve their younger brother, Arthur, from an orphanage in Belfast and bring him to join them. I agreed.

On returning to Georgetown, we left instructions for Paul

to fully supply them with all they would need before returning them to the plantation. We all coasted down to Charleston where they retrieved their personal belongings and said farewell to their shipmates.

If they needed advice, Mrs. Quick's overseer would be available for help. Money was deposited in the Cheraw bank to be used as needed. Johnson would come up river once a month to check on them and communicate their progress to James. I would return by early fall.

With things settled as well as we could make them, I returned to *Banshee* for the voyage home. I was so eager to return, I urged her onward in her journey by sheer force of will. There was much to do when I returned to Belfast.

3

IT WAS NON-STOP FROM Charleston to Belfast. The trades blew unchanging from the southwest, speeding us along. The current of the mighty Gulf Stream increased our true speed also. Rounding into Lough Belfast, we made short work of the trip to our home berth.

"Can you believe it, Thomas? Only eleven days from Charleston to Belfast! As sweet a journey as you ever saw." Mr. Clancy beamed.

"Aye. And not a day too soon to suit me. I have much to do before our next trip."

Word had passed along the shore that we were in the Lough, so Father was on the dock to meet us.

"Thomas, my son. You have survived to sail another day. Quickly now, lad. Tell me of your brothers, your journey, and what treasures you have brought to trade! And don't forget to tell me all about the Carolina wilderness."

Father had never been known as a patient man. As we walked to the company offices, he asked questions with every breath. We entered his office and sat over looking the harbor. His clerk brought tea and cakes. I told him of our experience with the Barbary pirates. Father's blue eyes bulged out of his weathered face.

"Ye did what?! Are ye mad? To take on three Barbary pirates is foolishness. *Banshee* can out sail any Algerian ever born. Why did ye not sail away?"

"Father, they had us trapped. Had it not been for Patrick Clancy's bravery, we would have lost *Banshee*, the cargo and the crew, myself included."

"Well, that is why we arm her so well for a merchant schooner. If ye could not flee, then fight like a good 'un!"

"Then do you forgive us, Father?"

"Aye, as long as I have the return of my ship and the safety of her cargo."

"And your seventh son?"

"Aye, there is that. But there are six more of ye!"

We laughed, and I gave him news of William and James. I went over the manifest with him to show how we had done with our trading. I gave him the details of the new timber ship, and that she was nearly ready to put to sea. Our longest discussion focused on the newly acquired land. I gave him a detailed description and our plans for developing it.

"My boy, ye are the blessed seventh son. Ye will do right well. The company will provide you a guaranteed income of 100 English pounds a year. If there is a profit, 25 percent will return to the company, 10 percent to your workers, and 65 percent for yourself. Are you agreeable?"

"Aye. Agreeable and anxious to be off. We are fortunate to have found young Cunningham. He will be a great asset, as will the other lads."

"Let's be off to home. Your mother will be glad to see you. Not too much about the pirates, Thomas. You know how she worries."

My safe return was adequately celebrated, and the cargo unloaded. Father calculated the profits to the farthing, paid the men their wages and bonuses. They would be kickin' up Bob's your uncle again tonight. Father had insisted the men have accounts for savings and investment, and sternly challenged them to save every penny they could spare. I suppose it was the Scots Presbyterian coming out in him. Some of the men had accumulated significant amounts. Patrick Clancy had been able to buy a nice small farm outside Belfast with two tenant farmers. McNamara owned a small tavern in Belfast, *Banshee*'s Daughter.

I spent my days in the company offices drafting plans and making lists of things we would need for the plantation. It occurred to me I had neglected planning my own future. I had sadly neglected my sweetheart, Priscella Alexander. I had called on her since my return a few times, but I had been too pre-occupied with the plantation. There was no excuse for it. I would go to see her that day. I drafted a note and had one of the office boys take it to her house. She returned a short reply that she was at leisure for dinner at her parent's home at six o'clock.

I left the office early to visit the barber for a shave and a haircut. Then I went home for a good scrubbing and put on my best shore-going clothes and shoes. I had the groom saddle a fine black horse. I arrived promptly at six o'clock with a bouquet of flowers and a brace of champagne bottles.

The doorman sent the groom to tend to my horse and invited me into the parlor. Miss Priscella was not down yet. I took tea with her parents as I waited. When she appeared at the top of the stairs, it was obvious that it had been worth the wait. Her long, auburn hair and brown eyes glowed in the light of the whale oil lamps. She was dressed in a dark green satin dress with a short necklace of pearls. Her smile brightened the room and stirred my heart! The dinner was delicious, the champagne excellent. But I hardly noticed as I was so completely distracted by Priscella.

After dinner, with a warm fire on the hearth, Priscella and I talked into the evening, sipping a fine sherry. I told her of my recent journey and the excitement encountered along the way. I groveled for forgiveness for my inattention. I told her of my plans for the plantation. I had known Priscella almost all of my life. I had been calling on her for over a year, although I had been gone several months during that time. Our relationship had been progressing steadily. I had known for some time that I wanted to take her for my wife. I took a deep breath, and asked her if I could approach her father to ask for her hand. She stared speechlessly at me. Had I overplayed my hand?

"Thomas Turner! Do you not know how I feel about you? I am honored that you would take me for a wife. I love you dearly. Of course you can ask my father."

I called upon him the next day at his office in the great spinning mill he owned. He did not seem surprised to see me. Perhaps Priscella had forewarned him of my intentions. He sent his clerk for a fine ruby port and a good local cheese. Even though I was certain he knew the reason for my visit, he waited for me to breech the topic. I told him of the plans for the plantation in the

Carolinas. He listened with intense interest. I finally approached the subject of Priscella. He feigned disinterest and doubts, but finally broke into a wide smile.

"Thomas, the answer is yes. You may marry Priscella. I have known you these many years and seen you grow into a fine young man. I know that you will be a good husband to her. I suggest that you have the proposed nuptials posted immediately."

"Mr. Alexander, I thank ye, sir. I promise to give her the best of all that I have to give."

"I know that ye will, Thomas. God bless ye both."

The proposed nuptials were posted, and the date set for one month from Saturday. This hindered my carefully laid plans, but in a wonderful way. Invitations were sent to family and friends, and all of *Banshee*'s crew and their families.

The fathers of both Zachary Hawkins and Dylan Caswell called on me at the shipping office. Both asked if I would be willing to take their sons with me to the Carolinas. They felt they stood a better chance of advancement there. Both boys were eager to go. I knew the boys well and did not hesitate to agree to take them with me. I promised to take good care of them. They would have the same offer as the other men: one and a half times their wages and a share in the profits. It was agreed.

As Priscella and the women in both families readied for the wedding, I continued making preparations for our migration. I found a good used mill that would grind wheat or corn using animal power to turn the millstones. I bought several fine rifled hunting muskets, and two double-barreled fowling pieces. I bought myself a beautiful double-barreled rifled musket in .45 caliber made by Joseph Manton of London. It was truly a work of art. I bought bullet molds, extra flints and two small kegs of fine gunpowder. The kegs were roughly three gallons each and fastened with copper hoops. I also found the most commonly needed repair parts for our weapons. I bought a plow with changeable plates that could be used for breaking new ground, cultivating, and listing rows. I bought a keg of nails, an assortment of good sturdy farm and hand tools, plus a double bladed saw for making uniform planks.

We would buy tea and household goods in Belfast. Priscella had asked that I buy some glass windows to build into our new home. I agreed and had them carefully packed for the voyage. We would take her cedar hope chest with us, but would buy or build the rest of our furniture there.

The packet brig brought news from William, James, and Paul Johnson. James had been to Cheraw twice to see how the work was progressing. Paul had been uniformly positive about the plantation, James agreed with Paul's assessment. The boys had made a camp near Phill's Creek. They had built a tight hut on a dry piece of ground. They were feeding themselves with the supplies they had taken with them and hunting. Mark had identified what he thought to be good acres for farming, and they were clearing the trees there. The trees were being saved for various uses. Some had been hewn square and were stacked to cure for building the cabin. The branches that were not suitable for the cabin were being used to start a fence above the flood line along Phill's Creek. Paul had helped them pick out another few acres that would be the best site for the cabin and out buildings. He thought they would have roughly ten acres cleared of timber by the time we arrived, pulling the stumps with the oxen. Keenan had put his froe to good use and had a large stack of wooden shingles piled up to cure. It appeared there would be enough to roof the house and the out buildings. They had dug a well and lined it with stone. The water was not too deep and was sweet and clear. They had built a stone foundation of 20x30 feet for the house set back from the road. Mrs. Quick's overseer had proven to be very helpful. Paul had taken them their pay, but they seemed to need little, and even less to buy with it. He was entirely satisfied with the progress. The office at Georgetown was progressing well. The spar and mast yard was busy. The rice mill should be operational by fall. The *Pride of Charleston* had sailed on her maiden voyage with a cargo of choice masts, spars and timber. It was planned that she would sail in convoy with *Banshee* on my return.

No one protested the banns and the wedding date approached rapidly. We were to be married by one of the Presbyterian elders from our home church. My brother, Edward, was to stand up with me. Priscella's sister, Elizabeth, would be her maid of honor. Her father was providing a generous dowry of 300 pounds sterling.

The appointed first Saturday of July arrived none too soon. I was smitten with Priscella and anxious to make her my wife. The wedding was at ten o'clock in the morning. There was a huge crowd, including the ship's crew, my father's farm tenants and all their families.

I was dressed in fine new clothes. Priscella was radiantly beautiful. We were beginning a life full of love, joy, triumph and tragedy. She would be at my side as we carved a new home out of the wilderness. I knew I had chosen a mate who would love me and stand by me, and I would give her the best of all I had. There was a great feast prepared with music and dancing. After a few hours, her father's carriage and matched black horses came to take us away. They delivered us to a beautiful small cottage in a grove of trees on the banks of a small stream on one of my father's farms. The cottage had been prepared for our stay. Two gentle horses were stabled next to the cottage for our use. We spent a quiet romantic week there together in peace and solitude. We caught trout in the stream and went for long rides in the countryside. Father had paid the wives of his tenants to provide us with a fresh basket of food for each day. We would remember this special time together for the rest of our lives.

With the honeymoon over, we stayed at the Alexander's home. The *Pride of Charleston* made her grand entry. The other ship owners gawked at her size, design and good handling. Her cargo caused quite a stir among the ship yards. They paid top price for her masts, spars and timber.

The *Banshee* was loaded with those things destined for the plantation and other cargo. She and our companion vessel were in ballast with iron and lead bars. The immense hold of *Pride* was filled with a tremendous volume of trade goods bound for the colonies and the islands. Edward would be traveling aboard *Pride* to take up his post managing the new office in Georgetown.

Our crew was largely the same, less the four we had left in South Carolina. They had been replaced by men I did not know. Zachary and Dylan brought extra goods in their sea bags and chests as their parents bid them farewell. The boys tried valiantly to hold their tears, but their mothers' sobs had them crying too. The Alexander's came to see Priscella off, and tears marked their parting. We had located little Arthur Perkins who was glad to leave the orphanage to go to his brothers.

A colonial sailing master, Jedediah Williams, commanded the *Pride*. He was a taut sailor, and Mr. Clancy seemed to respect his abilities. As ship's master for both vessels, I advised Mr. Clancy all cargo was aboard.

"Mr. Williams, is that floating lumber yard ready to set sail?"

"Aye, aye, sir. Hope she don't leave you behind"

"Patrick, have the men cast off the moorings. Van Pelt, set the jib and bring her head around."

Banshee gently turned away from the dock, catching the southerly breeze. *Pride* did also, but more slowly due to her great size.

"Van Pelt, fore and main sails!"

"McNamara, heading north northeast."

Banshee responded and moved gently out into the harbor, with *Pride* following in our wake.

"Topsails if you please, Mr. Van Pelt."

As the topsails were set and drawing, *Banshee* heeled gently away from the wind and picked up speed. *Pride* set fore, main and mizzen topsails, and the mizzen spanker. It was obvious she was no slug. This August 1, 1749, our odyssey began. Far across the Atlantic lay the wilderness that was to be our new home.

4

DYLAN'S VOICE WAS
urgent as he banged on my cabin door.

"Mr. Turner! Mr. Turner! Mr. Clancy says to
come now, sir! Mr. Turner! It's an emergency, sir!"

I hurriedly pulled on my clothes, and reassured
Priscella it probably wasn't anything too serious. As I
saw Brian Clancy's face, I knew it must be bad.

"Thomas, we have a problem. The glass
is dropping fast. We are in for some very nasty
weather."

"What is different this time? We have weathered
many a storm together."

"Aye, that we have. But look to the southeast
and tell me what you see?"

There was not a star to be seen. The southeastern
sky was alive with distant flashes of lightning across
a vast expanse of the sky. We had left the Azores
two days ago. The sailing had been good. But earlier

today, we had seen a large cloud bank forming in the southeast. This time of the year in the Atlantic was hurricane season. The dropping glass meant a major storm was near. The faster and farther it dropped, the more dangerous the situation.

"It looks to be a hurricane, Brian."

"Aye, and a bad one!"

"We are far from some rock-bound coast. Do we ride it out?"

"Aye. I'll signal *Pride* our intentions. Patrick, make the signal to strike topmasts. Reduce sail. Keep station astern. Fire a gun to leeward to make sure they see our lanterns."

"*Pride* acknowledges, sir."

"Van Pelt, strike the topmasts on deck and secure them. Take in all the sail except the jib. Double lash the boats and the guns."

"Mr. Moore, check the hold. We want no cargo breaking loose. Check the pumps. We may well need them!"

We could now hear the thunder coming from the storm. The lightning was continuous. The wind increased steadily, as did the waves. The glass continued to drop ominously. I went below to tell Priscella what was happening. She was frightened, but brave.

As the night wore on, warm rain began to fall. It came in fitful squalls at first, then in driving horizontal sheets. The rain seemed to have replaced the air. We wrapped tarpaulins across our faces to allow a dry space to breathe. Visibility dropped to nothing. Clancy had a swivel gun fired to leeward every few minutes, and we could hear *Pride*'s response. We occasionally could see the muzzle flash. The rigging vibrated with the increasing wind until it was making an audible humming. The waves increased until they were breaking over the stern. The hold and hatches had been battened down, but not all of the breaking sea could be kept out. Zachary and Dylan turned the crank on the pump relentlessly. The pump was throwing a full, steady stream of water over the side. McNamara and Van Pelt both had the wheel. They had to keep *Banshee* running before the wind. If they lost control of the wheel, if the steering ropes parted or the rudder failed, *Banshee* would turn broadside to the wind and waves and capsize. Men stood by in the stern below decks ready to fit and handle a manual tiller if the ropes parted. Other hands stood by on the deck with sharpened axes to cut away any falling rigging that might foul the ship. Every man and boy had a job and there would be no rest until the storm abated.

The wind in the rigging rose to a higher pitch. The lightning flashed continuously in blinding explosions all around the ship. The thunder was deafening. *Banshee* pitched like a horse jumping a gate. I had lashed Priscella in her cot. She was deathly pale and clutching the sides with a death grip. Little Arthur Perkins was helping the boys at the pump, too tired to cry anymore. John Cook brought sliced cold beef and cheese to each of us. He then took a turn at the pump, letting first one, then another take a brief break to eat.

We could no longer fire the swivel gun anymore due to the severity of the storm. Nor could we hear a gun from *Pride* or see her top lanterns.

The sky lightened gradually in the east hiding a water-logged sun, but it was still almost as dark as it had been all night. The wind dropped slightly, and the waves lessened a little. The center of the lightning was now away to the northwest of us, over the starboard bow. Mr. Moore, Conner McLean and I relieved the exhausted boys at the pumps. The three of us could manage alone for a while. They fell asleep on the deck, oblivious to the storm's declining fury.

By mid-morning, sunlight would occasionally penetrate the clouds. The wind died to a manageable gale. The waves were still tall and wide, but no longer broke over the stern. The rain died away to occasional squalls. The storm had passed us, and we were alive. I went below to check on Priscella, who had finally fallen asleep of exhaustion and fear. I wakened her gently to let her know the worst was over. She smiled and tugged at the lashings. Once freed, she sat up and gave me a tight hug, then fell back to sleep.

We fired a six-pounder with a full powder charge to leeward. Far astern over the port quarter, we heard an answering gun. Even though we could not see her, we knew *Pride* had survived, too.

"Mr. Van Pelt, I'll leave ye alone at the helm while Patrick and I survey the damage. Ask Mr. Moore to sound the hold."

I accompanied them in assessing the ship. There was only minor damage. I joined Mr. Moore in the hold to check the cargo. The well had only 14 inches of water. The pumps could clear that in twenty minutes. One box of ready-made clothes was smashed, but could be salvaged. A chest of tools had the lid torn off, but the tools could be dried and oiled and the lid replaced. Dylan was sent aloft to see if he could locate *Pride*. He spotted her about a league to the southeast, and had all her masts standing and a jib sail set.

"Dylan, run up the signal for 'Do you need assistance?' and wait for her reply."

"She signals 'No assistance'."

"Send 'Make more sail, close on flag'."

"Sir, she responds 'Understand' and is setting her staysails and spanker."

"Good, come down, and bring your brother from the mast. I smell hot food in the galley!"

John Cook and Zachary soon served steaming bowls of oatmeal with butter and molasses. This was all washed down with rum mixed with hot water and a squeeze of lime. It tasted like a feast to us. I carried a bowl below to Priscella, who ate it gladly.

By noon, *Pride* was once more in our wake, and we had all plain sail set. We would wait until we were a bit more recovered to replace the topmasts. The storm had blown us in the direction of Barbados, and we sighted its inhospitable eastern shore three days after the storm. Even as unlovely as it was, I was delighted to see land. Priscella came on deck to watch us round the southern end of the island as we made for Bridgetown. We refilled our water casks and renewed our supply of perishable foods. The storm had veered to the northeast, leaving Barbados with much needed heavy rains. The next morning we pushed on for Jamaica.

In two days, the southeast corner of Jamaica was in view and we made our way west to Kingston. The harbor pilot guided *Banshee* and *Pride* right up to the company dock. As the ships were moored, I climbed down from *Banshee* and Edward from *Pride*.

"Rough going for a while there baby brother."

"Naught but a light gale for an old tar, Edward."

"Thomas! Edward! Well met, brothers!"

"William. Let me fetch my bride to meet ye."

I returned to *Banshee*'s side to help Priscella onto the wharf. She had regained her looks after the storm, and I could see she had dressed especially nice to meet William.

"Priscella, may I introduce you to my brother, William. William, this is Priscella."

"It is my pleasure to meet the seventh son's wife. You are lovely as a flower, sister. Thomas, I see that ye have chosen well, and married above ye from what I can see."

We exchanged pleasantries as we headed for the company offices. William had known Priscella's father in Belfast. He sent his clerk for tea and cakes while we visited. He asked the details of the storm, which Edward and I readily supplied. He had heard of no loss of any of the other company ships, but a Portuguese merchant ship had been lost with all hands west of the Azores.

Our agent and McNamara were already unloading the cargo marked for Kingston, the hold was restowed and the new cargo in place. It took longer to unload *Pride*, as she carried such a large volume of goods. Her hoists and booms made it easier on the crew as less cargo had to be man handled to the dock. She had suffered little and had not lost any cargo in the storm. Her new cargo was quickly put into place for the next leg of our journey.

William invited the sailing master of *Pride*, Jedediah Williams, along with Brian Clancy, Edward, Priscella and me to dinner at his home. We enjoyed a wonderful meal and caught up on family and company news.

The next morning we began the passage through the Santo Domingo Strait. We anchored in good holding ground for the night. By the following morning, we were tediously threading our way through the Bahamas Passage. Twice, strange sail appeared, but retreated to their hiding places after spotting our size and armament. We kept the lead going constantly in the bows to watch for shoals or reefs. A sailor with sharp eyes was stationed in the foremast crosstrees to watch for changes in the color of the water and another in the mainmast trees to watch for unwelcome visitors.

Just as we were clearing the last of the passage, a fluke of wind pushed *Pride* a bit west of the channel. She grounded lightly on hard sand. She was too heavy for *Banshee* to tow off the sand bar. Using *Pride*'s boats, they set out her kedge anchor far beyond her bow in good holding ground. Her crew strained at the great capstan until the slack was out of the heavy cable. With a few more turns, it was taut as a fiddle string. Hands were now at both the upper and lower capstan bars. It was a contest of sheer muscle and gears against the sand bar. The cable was rigid, and nothing moved. The men strained with all their might against the bars. Finally, there was a click of a pawl as a few inches were gained. Pushing even harder, the pawl clicked again and again. The sand swirled from the sand bar as the huge ship inched forward. The clanking of the pawl increased steadily, and the *Pride* was once again afloat. They recovered their anchor, and we were soon again on our way.

We made an overnight stop in Savannah, as we could not reach Charleston before dark. The hurricane had brushed the coast there, but there had been no major damage. By daybreak we cleared the Outer Banks, and made our way north to Charleston. By early afternoon, the harbor entrance was in sight. The harbor pilot guided us in to the company wharf. James was expecting us and I introduced him to Priscella. He welcomed her warmly and invited us to supper at his home, where we repeated the tale of our passage. The men were caught up on their pay and given shore leave. Priscella and I spent the night ashore at James and Lucy's gracious home.

In the morning all the cargo for Charleston was unloaded and new cargo stowed aboard. The *Pride* would proceed to Georgetown to take on a load of spars, masts and timber. *Banshee* would deliver us there, where we would proceed up the Pee Dee to our new home in the South Carolina wilderness.

5

I HAD MADE MANY
voyages to the Carolinas as my father's representative.
This time it was different. As I set foot on the wharf
at Georgetown, I was filled with a sense of awe. It
struck me that this was a new beginning. It was a new
beginning of something much more than another
family business venture. It was the beginning of my
married life, my own family. It was the beginning of a
new way of life where the old hatreds and prejudices
that had followed my family for generations could
be left behind. It would not matter that I was Scots
or Irish, Catholic, Anglican or Presbyterian. I did not
know with a certainty what the future held, but I was
so excited I felt myself trembling. I held tightly to
Priscella's hand. She looked at me and smiled. She
understood.

I helped her down onto the dock, and introduced
Edward and Priscella to Paul Johnson. Zachary,

Dylan, and Arthur gathered their few personal belongings on the dock. They were starting new lives, too. Paul gave us the latest news of the plantation. In the four months I had been gone, Mark, Logan, Sean, and Keenan had accomplished more than I had expected. They had completed the rail fence along Phill's Creek above the high water line. They had set the foundation for the cabin, from the sleepers to the puncheons. The logs for the rest of the cabin had cured. They were now measured, cut, squared and notched for assembly. There was a large pile of oak shingles stacked, cured and ready to roof the cabin and out buildings. They had cleared the timber from ten acres. They had removed the stumps from about half of it. There was a small sweet spring south of the cabin that trickled its way down to the creek. With advice from Mrs. Quick's overseer they had built a spring house of mortared stone. It caught the spring water at its source and ran it through stone troughs along the walls of the spring house before it returned on its way to the creek. It would be wonderful to keep foods fresh longer, and to keep the water fresh and sweet and cool.

I was amazed they had done so much. I could not wait to get there. The remaining trade cargo aboard *Banshee* was unloaded. Then all the goods heading to the plantation were loaded onto a large scow for our trip up river. We bought a barrel of flour, another of corn meal, a large sack of dried beans, five sacks of dried corn for the animals, a quantity of lard, some cured hams, a barrel of smoked bacon packed in salt, several crock ware jars of molasses, a large round of cheese, a basket of fresh cabbages, two crates of potatoes, and another of sweet potatoes. We bought a young milk cow due to calve in the fall, and another horse similar to the one we had left with the boys. We included tea, salt, sugar and spices. Limited supplies would be available in Cheraw. When necessary, we would return to Georgetown for those things that were not locally available.

The breeze favored our trip up the Great Pee Dee. The oarsmen laid into their long sweeps with a will, chanting their river song as they worked. Edward and Paul were going with us to inspect the plantation and return the scow to Georgetown. Zachary, Dylan and Arthur took in every sight along the river. The rice fields along the lower river were ripening. Sugar cane harvest was in progress. The day was beautiful and mild. With the help of the wind and the strength of the rowers, we made Cheraw before dark. We tied the scow up at Cheraw Landing. Paul would stay with our goods, the boat and the boys. Edward, Priscella and I paid the ferryman to take us across to Cheraw. The wagon coach took us up the hill to the hotel. It was two stories tall, built of finished lumber painted white, with glass windows. We took our belongings to our rooms to freshen up before supper. The rooms were supplied with finely crafted furniture, feather mattresses, down pillows and fine bed linens. The dining room was excellent. Priscella especially enjoyed the comfort of the hotel after our Spartan accommodations during our voyage.

Early the next morning, we paid a visit to the Bank of Cheraw to talk with our banker. Our line of credit on the Planter's and Merchant's Bank of Charleston was well established. We left the hotel and took the wagon coach back down the hill. The ferryman responded to the large bell we rang, and quickly transported us to the far bank. Cheraw was the end of the navigable part of the Pee Dee, as only shortly above the river was a waterfall. The boys from the plantation had arrived with the wagon and oxen, leading the other horse. We loaded as much as we could into the wagon, and led the milk cow tied behind. We would return the next day to retrieve the rest of our things. The ferryman could be trusted to watch over them in our absence.

Sean and Logan were delighted to see their brother, Arthur, whom they called "Artie." It was good to see all of them again. All four of them were taller and stronger. They spent much of the trip to the plantation quizzing Zach and Dylan about the hurricane. They, in turn, had many stories to tell of their time in the Carolina wilderness. We arrived by late afternoon. The pace of the gentle oxen was steady but slow. They had chosen a perfect location for the cabin. It would command a wonderful view of the crops, forest and the road. As the boys unloaded the wagon, Edward and I took a ride along the creek to inspect the fence. They had done a good job building it, and it was above the flood line where it would not have to be rebuilt after every heavy rain. Their camp was neat and clean. The spring house was well designed and well built. They had a haunch of venison cooling there. The fence they had built along the road was faultless. I had never seen a better one. Obviously, they were taking pride in their work.

The cabin was laid out in the dog-trot fashion. It would connect both twenty foot by twenty foot cabins with a ten foot wide breezeway. The north cabin would be divided into two rooms. The southern portion would be our great room, kitchen and dining room. There would be four rooms of equal size on the second story, accessed by stairs from the back porch. The bottom story would have deep porches the width of the cabin facing east and west. The logs had been squared, measured, notched and numbered awaiting assembly. Keenan had made a large number of locust pegs to fasten the logs. The fireplace and chimney had already been built in place with mortared stone.

Our first night, Zachary roasted the venison in the lonely fireplace after rubbing it well with salt and pepper. We enjoyed our first meal there. All seven of the boys crowded into their hut and talked the night away. We left the perishable items in the wagon under a tarp. We placed tarps on the ground for the rest of us, with another tarp draped over a pole to form a roof. The weather was fair and mild. The sounds of the wilderness could be heard most of the night, with owls, night hawks, and other wild animals adding their voices. I had never heard the odd and eerie sound of coyotes in the night, but Paul explained to us what it was. The howl of a wolf and its answering hunting companion was more frightening than interesting. Priscella snuggled closer, and I checked my rifle. My mind raced with excitement and plans most of the night. I was excited as a little boy with his first pony.

The next morning, all three Perkins boys took Paul and Edward back to Cheraw Landing. The slaves loaded the heavier items and the mill into the wagon. Edward said he would try to return in about a month to check on us. The boys returned late afternoon. There was much to be done.

Before it was dark, we started handling logs into place. Keenan's advance preparation made it go quickly. As each log was settled into place, high spots were trimmed off with an adze. A hand drill and bit was used to make a hole through each corner where a locust peg was hammered into place and trimmed flat. This would keep the logs from shifting. We concentrated on building the south part of the cabin. By dark, we had all the logs in place up about seven feet high.

The next day, a four inch thick door frame was drilled and

pegged into place. We would cut out window openings later. We then began raising the north side. It was completed by nightfall, including two door openings framed into place. That night, the boys crowded into their hut again. I rigged a pole across the unfinished walls of the south half, and stretched a canvas across it to make a shelter for Priscella and me. The next day we fitted six inch square floor joists in the pre-cut slots on the top log. These would eventually support the upper floor. Two inch thick floor boards were planed smooth on one side and carefully fastened in place with pegs. Keenan had taught Logan how to drill the holes and set the pegs. With both of them working, the work went quickly. That afternoon Mrs. Quick came for a welcoming visit. I introduced Priscella to her, as well as the boys she had not met.

"I have brought ye a venison stew with potatoes, carrots and onions, a pan of cornbread, a bit of butter, and a pitcher of fresh milk."

Priscella smiled. "Thank ye, neighbor Quick. This will save me from cooking for these hungry men. They are working up quite a fierce appetite these days. I hope to come see you soon and return your pitcher, pots and pans."

"Aye. I would like that. There are few enough women about these parts. I look forward to your company."

We all enjoyed the stew and corn bread. The milk was a rare treat, as was the butter. We feasted that night and slept soundly.

Our work on the cabin was now slowed by the height at which we worked. We were able to lean the logs to be raised against the side of the existing wall. We fastened the upper end to a heavy rope run across the top to the oxen on the other side.

At the signal, we heaved up on the bottom end while Dylan led the oxen forward, dragging the log up to the second story. We were only able to raise the south second story wall to waist high that day, plus the wall over the breezeway. The next day, we repeated the process with similar results. Now we reached a dilemma. We could not raise the timbers any higher with the oxen.

I had an idea that I thought might work. We would try to build a sheer tackle like we used to raise a new mast. We cut two tall, straight pine trees that were about eight inches in diameter, and sawed off all the branches and peeled the bark. We notched the two logs near the upper end, fastened them together with a large solid locust peg, and reinforced it with rope lashings. Just under the inverted V we fastened a block and tackle and worked our rope through it. We then anchored the bottom ends a few feet out from the cabin walls. The block and tackle now stood several feet above the side walls. We ran the end of the rope out to the oxen on the far side of the cabin. The near end we fastened securely to the notch in the log to be lifted. Once over half the length of the log was over the top, the boys on the second story would pull the top end of the log down onto the upper floor as Dylan backed the oxen a few steps. It worked well, but was slow going.

With our nautical gear in place, we were slowly and steadily able to raise all the logs needed to complete the upper sides, and raise the rafters to the second floor. Once the rafters were on the second floor, we could man handle them into place. They had been notched and drilled before they were raised into place. A peg was inserted once they were in position. The roof had a steep pitch of about forty-five degrees. Below each peak, a two inch thick board was pegged into place to strengthen the roof. Once all the rafters were secured, sawed planks two inches thick were nailed into place on two foot centers. This made the roof strong and rigid. The long oak shingles were overlapped and nailed onto these cross boards. Soon, we had an enclosed cabin.

The openings for the precious glass windows we had brought with us across the Atlantic were cut out of the log walls and frames custom made for each window. The upstairs was divided into four rooms with a central hallway, and the lower north room was divided into two rooms. The doors were made of planed wood. Sean made metal hinges, handles and latches for all the doors, and for the shutters we built for the windows. The carefully squared and fitted logs fit so well that almost no chinking was required.

Our cabin was spacious and tight against the elements. The windows, such a wonderful luxury, allowed light to flood into the rooms. They could be raised or lowered to adjust the temperature of the cabin, and the shutters could be closed for extra protection during bad weather. For a log cabin in the wilderness, it was a palace.

Keenan built a large dining table and benches. He also made a side-board for Priscella's kitchen utensils, with circular openings to hold metal basins for washing dishes. He made a few extra chairs for the great room, and enough beds for everyone from carefully pegged wood frames and tightly stretched rope. Priscella made pillow cases and mattresses with cotton ticking we had brought with us. She stuffed them with Spanish moss that had been smoked to remove any "little critters." The beds were fitted with cotton sheets and wool blankets. The three

Perkins boys shared one room upstairs. Keenan and Mark shared another, and Zachary and Dylan shared a third room. Priscella and I took one of the downstairs rooms for our own. The other rooms were used as a sewing room for Priscella and an office by me, although each had an extra bed in case of visitors. We had built an outside staircase under the back porch to access the upstairs hallway. Our house was completed, and it felt like home already. But our work in the wilderness had hardly begun.

6

THE FALL OF 1749 WAS
kind to us. The weather was mild, and the fall rains
were slow and gentle. We met the neighbors. To the
southeast were the homes of W.W. and Jonathan
Irby. They were pleasant, and Priscella enjoyed
their wives. Their plantations were about five years
ahead of ours. They showed me their farms and out
buildings. Their indigo had already been harvested
and processed for the year. Only the bush like stalks
remained to bring the next year's crop. The tobacco
was drying in the barns with slow maple wood fires
smoldering on the earthen floors. They explained the
smoking killed the tobacco weevils which could ruin
tobacco in shipping.

We always enjoyed the Widow Quick, whose
name fit her wit and personality. She was especially
helpful to Priscella with her knowledge of running a
household in the Carolina backwoods. On the road

to Cheraw, just west of our property, was Mrs. Harrington, who was kind, quiet and reserved. Although she did not tell us, Mrs. Quick said Mr. Harrington was deceased. To the east of our cabin, the road ran half a day's travel to Brightsville. But not far to the east, a road turned back to the south. On this road lived the Grants and the Smiths. We did not know them well. Mr. Grant was said to have some of the finest livestock in the area. I planned to visit him in the spring.

The acres that Mark had selected were excellent. It was a rich clay loam, dark and fertile. We spent much of the fall removing stumps. We dug down as deeply as we could, and sawed or chopped off all the roots within reach. We wrapped chains around the top portion of the stumps, and harnessed them to the gentle oxen. As they laid into their yokes, we pried under the stumps with long hickory poles. We dragged the stumps to the edge of the field. Keenan inspected each stump for curved or angled pieces that could be used for specific carpentry needs. The logs were set aside for our further building needs.

When the last of the stumps were pulled, we set about the ten acres with our breaking plow pulled by the oxen. Dylan, who was emerging as our herdsman, led the oxen, while Logan wrestled with the plow. Zachary followed behind them with a spike-tooth harrow Keenan and Sean had built, drawn by the two horses. The freshly turned ground had to be harrowed almost immediately to prevent the large clumps of earth from becoming rock-hard clods. Arthur followed behind picking up roots and rocks that came to the surface.

Once the ten acres were as ready as we could make them for spring planting, we started to clear an adjacent area for our out buildings. The first would be our great stock and feed barn.

It was two stories tall, with a hay loft in the upper level. There was a tightly sealed feed room, and an area for tools and tack. Roosts and laying boxes were built along the ground floor walls for the chickens we hoped to buy in the spring. The barn had two large swinging doors that Keenan and Sean had designed to swing without sagging. When the doors were opened the wagon could be driven through the barn to unload. There were wooden windows at each stall for ventilation. The windows closed tightly enough to keep out predators.

Next we built our blacksmith and carpenters workshop just off the road. Next to the shop we set up the mill for later use. A tobacco drying barn with slatted sides was built next to the stock barn. It was built large enough to handle much more tobacco than we would grow for several years. Near the house we built a stout smokehouse of squared logs. There was a gap of about an inch left between each log to allow ventilation. The smokehouse was built solidly enough to keep out any bear in the area. Finally, we built a bear-proof hog pen that could accommodate six sows and a boar. The Smith's had shown us how they had built theirs. The pen was far enough from the house to keep the odor away, but near enough to keep a close eye on the hogs. The timber for these buildings cleared another two acres. We pulled the stumps, plowed and harrowed the ground. We sowed our first seed on these acres, oats for a spring harvest. With the first rain it jumped from the ground. It was green and lush all winter.

Early in 1750, we had gone deer hunting, as we wanted some fresh meat. Deer were plentiful and fat due to the heavy acorn crop. Keenan had dropped a nice doe at the edge of a thicket. As he and Zachary were dressing the deer, a large black bear crashed through the brush right on top of them.

He swatted Zachary aside with one huge paw. He turned on Keenan and knocked him to the ground. Seeing the danger the boys were in, I charged toward the bear yelling. Enraged, he made straight for me. His shoulders and head were low to the ground. His mighty hindquarters were raised, propelling him faster than I dreamed a bear could run. At about 75 feet, I raised my double barreled rifle, and put a .45 caliber ball deep in his chest. He stumbled, roared violently and continued his head-long charge. I fired a second shot at about 25 feet. My blood ran cold as I saw the bullet sink deep within his huge chest, and the enraged beast still charged. I dropped the rifle and pulled a flintlock pistol from my belt. I cocked and fired, only to see the bullet deflected from his thick skull. He paused to shake his great head in anger and pain. He rose up on his powerful hind legs. He stood a foot taller than me! He let out a great roar. I pulled out my second pistol and fired at point blank range into his chest. He shrieked in violent rage. He reached out with his mighty right paw and knocked me to the ground. As I watched in frozen horror, his legs folded beneath him and he collapsed next to me on the ground.

I was trembling so hard, I could not get to my feet. I rolled over and vomited up the fear within me. I finally staggered to my feet and wobbled to check on Zach and Keenan. Both were dazed, but not seriously hurt. They had great bruised paw prints where the bear had hit them. The sound of the shots had brought the rest of our party. I was still shaking so much I could not reload my gun, so I passed it to Sean to reload for me. My throat was so dry I croaked when I tried to talk. They looked in awe at the scene around them. Keenan recovered his wits enough to sit up. The others helped him field dress his doe. He reloaded his rifle while they worked with their knives. Sean and Logan began to field dress the bear.

Mark and Dylan ran back to the farm and hitched a wooden sled to both horses. They brought a cask of water and a dipper gourd. They also brought Artie, who couldn't wait to see the bear. It took all of us to wrestle the great beast onto the sled. The horses shied and pranced in their fear of the dead bear. Dylan stroked their necks and spoke softly to them in Irish. We estimated the bear to weigh better than four hundred pounds. We also loaded the doe onto the sled, which looked tiny by comparison. Zachary was standing next to the horses, still dazed. He walked holding on to the harness. The horses pulled with a will, but in rough places we had to push the sled.

Artie broke into an animated long story in Irish to Logan and Sean. They interpreted for my benefit. "Brian Boru, the first high king of Ireland, was returning from hunting red stags with his men. The great bear of all time set upon his party, shaking off their spears like splinters. The devil beast stood on his hind legs, roaring out a challenge to King Brian. The bear stood nine feet tall and weighed a thousand pounds, so help him St. Patrick. He charged the king, knocking him down and slinging his sword away. But King Brian drew his great dagger and sliced the bear's throat. The monstrously huge beast died upon King Brian, who was only rescued when some peasants rolled the bear from his breast. From that day forward, his banner was a great bear on a green field. Oh, Artie says he made the peasants lairds of the realm and rich as kings, too."

"Ah, now my Irish lad. That is the great story of all time. Do ye think m' bear would measure up to that of King Brian?"

"Beggin' your pardon, your honor. Your bear is sure a

great fierce beast, but I believe King Brian's bear must have been bigger by far!"

We laughed as we continued through the forest to home. The young men were given the job of butchering the bear and the deer. We ate bear ribs and venison loin that night. Even at supper, my hands were still shaking so that I had to use both hands to hold my mug. I never told Priscella or the boys how terrified I really had been.

The salted and smoked bear meat and venison lasted for a few weeks. It was a while before I went hunting again, and even then had to force myself to go the next time.

That March, just before spring had arrived, a band of Cheraw Indians arrived at our plantation to visit. The neighbors had earlier told me that the Cheraw were peaceable and good neighbors. I had nothing to trade, but shared a meal with them. They sought work in the summer hoeing the fields, and helping with harvest in the fall. They spoke passably good English, and presented me with a nice freshly killed turkey. Their leader's Cheraw name I could not pronounce, but he said the white men called him Tom Red Hat for the red leather hat he wore. We invited him to come back in June and see what work we might have.

7

BY LATE MARCH, WE HAD
a total of fourteen acres cleared and plowed. This
included four acres of oats, which were already knee
high. All fourteen acres had a rail fence around them
to keep our livestock out. They had the run of the rest
of the place, as the perimeter was completely fenced.
We let them out in the morning after feeding them,
let them graze during the day, and put them back in
the barn at night. The milk cow and both oxen calved.
We milked all three, but left plenty for the calves to
grow fat.

I rode over to Mr. Grant's farm with Dylan in
the wagon. I negotiated with him to buy a young
gentle bull. I also bought a fine wool ram and a dozen
similar young ewes. I bought a young boar and three
young sows, plus a rooster and twenty pullets. We
led the bull behind the wagon, and loaded the rest in
the wagon box. Keenan had made removable sides to

raise it high enough to transport livestock. We had the pleasure of the chickens' company in two wooden crates on the wagon seat between us. We put the hogs in the bear-proof pen filled with sawdust. We kept the new animals in the barn long enough for them to realize this is where the food was to be found. After a few days we turned them out with the other animals without incident. The chickens roamed as they pleased, but quickly discovered the roosts and nesting boxes.

Mark proved to be an asset. His education under his father was invaluable. He filled in many of the blanks that had worried me about the farm. He also acted as my clerk in keeping accounts. At times, I could see a far away look of loss in his eyes. I guessed that he was missing his family.

He rode with me to see Mr. Irby, who had done well with his indigo. I needed to buy indigo seed to plant two acres, and enough tobacco seed to plant another two acres. The indigo seed looked like very small purple English peas. Indigo seed sold on par with silver by weight, but the finished indigo dye sold on par with gold! He said I would need sixteen ounces of seed, so I paid him sixteen Spanish dollars. The tobacco seed was small and brown. He said I would need about a pound of seed, which cost me five more dollars. We also bought seed corn and wheat, Irish potatoes for planting, and sweet potatoes. He gave me various seeds for the garden. He offered to help us get started anyway he could.

When we returned, Mark gave Keenan the dimensions for large cold frames to be built on the south side of the house. Sean made hinges for the frames and latches for the lids to keep the skunks, raccoons and possums from eating the tender plants. The lids were covered with thin oil-tanned deerskin. It would allow some light to penetrate on days when it was too cold to open the frame, and would keep the heat in the frames at night. Logan filled the frames with the finest soil on the plantation, carefully screening it for rocks, roots and debris.

By early April, Mark and Zachary spent hours on their knees planting the precious indigo and tobacco seeds in the cold frames. They carefully watered the seeds with a watering can especially made to gently mist the seeds without disturbing them. If the day was warm, the frames were opened to give the plants more light and keep them from getting too hot. They left them closed on cold days, and on all but the warmest nights. Soon, delicate fern-like indigo plants were emerging, as were the more robust appearing tobacco seedlings.

While we waited for the seedlings to grow hardy enough to transplant, we planted the corn. Logan used the horses to lay off rows. The soil had already been worked, so we didn't need the extra strength of the oxen. The horses could cover the ground much faster than the lumbering bovines. Zach, Dylan, and Artie walked behind the horses planting the seed with sticks. They patted the ground over each seed with their hands to settle the soil.

Planting potatoes was similar. The best Irish and sweet potatoes were selected and cut into pieces containing one robust "eye" each. As Logan laid off the rows, the other three planted behind him.

By May it was warm enough to transplant the indigo and tobacco seedlings. Mark gently lifted the individual plants and carefully laid them into flat trays Keenan had built. Mark and Zachary personally transplanted them into the field. Dylan and Artie placed shingles on the north and west sides of the indigo plants to shield them from a chilly north wind or hot westerly sunlight. Sean and Logan came behind and watered each plant. It took a week to plant two acres of indigo. But it was a perennial and shouldn't have to be replanted. We took turns at night keeping the varmints scared away until the plants were a little bigger.

The tobacco was set out in a similar manner the next week, but without the protection of the shingles. It was a hardier type of plant. The animal didn't seem especially attracted to the tobacco plants. I later came to understand that once the indigo plants had any size to them, the smell of the plants repelled almost anything.

While we had been preoccupied with the field crops, Priscella had been planting the garden, often with help from the younger three boys. She also planted a small herb garden next to the cabin, and transplanted some apple, pear, and peach seedlings Mrs. Quick had given her. Whoever had night guard on the indigo also had to watch the two acre garden.

By mid-June we cut our first crop of oats on the farm, our first produce. We bound it into sheaves and carried them near the barn to thrash the seeds from the stalks. We carefully collected the grain and stored it in large barrels Keenan and Sean had made and put them in the feed room. We gathered up the sweet oat straw and put it in the loft for winter fodder.

My brothers, James and Edward, came to visit in July. They brought a letter from Father and news from home and abroad. Their trip up the Pee Dee had not been very pleasant. The wind had been foul for using a sail the whole way, and the oarsmen had to row against a stronger current than usual due to recent rains. They had to heave to for the night at Snow Island. The mosquitoes had descended on them in humming clouds of annoyance. They had brought mosquito netting for everyone, but no one got much sleep. They had rented horses at the landing and ridden in before supper.

"Thomas, the Pee Dee River in July is the colonial version of the River Styx. The shade of your porch and this spring water are very welcome relief. Edward and I are glad to see ye again."

"Aye! It is good to see the both of ye. When ye have rested, I want to show ye what we have done."

Mark joined the three of us on our inspection. The crops had been cultivated before the last rain. The rows were free of weeds, and the crops were thriving. The indigo and tobacco were waist high, and the corn was at least head high. The lush potatoes looked like Ireland. They were amazed at the fencing, garden, crops, livestock, out buildings and cabin. Priscella cooked a special supper of fresh vegetables, fried chicken, biscuits and freshly churned butter. After supper, we sat on the porch and enjoyed the breeze and caught up on news. Father's farms were doing well, and the shipping and trade business was thriving as usual. The spar, mast and timber yard was booming. The *Pride of Charleston* had proven so successful, a sister ship was being built in the Belfast shipyards. *Banshee* was still flying across the Atlantic, as were the other two schooners.

I told them our bear story, and showed them the tanned hide on the floor in my bedroom. I described the plentiful wildlife that we saw so often and provided us with so much meat.

I suggested to them that we consider making our plantation a trade center for the area, as it was so far to Cheraw or Brightsville. We could be a collecting point for produce to be shipped downriver, and we could be a local supplier of staples and hardware. They liked the idea and would put it to Father.

They had brought with them a small keg of gunpowder, a keg of nails, as well as a barrel each of flour, sugar and salt. They also brought bolts of heavy canvas duck for work clothes, cotton, linen and woolen cloth. They had left all of this for us to retrieve from the landing, plus five great kettles to process the indigo. When they got ready to go back, the boys and I took the wagon and horses and traveled with them to the scow they had left at the landing where we claimed our freight.

Mark and I selected a rolling part of the property that would not be suitable for crops to use as improved pasture. It already had a fair amount of grass and clover growing among the trees. Between other jobs, the boys cleared the underbrush, which they piled and burned. They saved the ashes to scatter on the stubble of the oat field. The pine trees were cut, trimmed and dragged to just above the flood line on the creek. When we had accumulated enough, we would raft them downstream to Georgetown. We left the stumps in place, much to everyone's delight. We left the hardwood trees undisturbed. By fall, the grass and other pasture plants were growing thickly in the twenty acre meadow. A tiny spring-fed stream provided water there, and it quickly became a favorite place of our livestock.

In September, the corn was ready to pick. The oxen pulled the wagon and the horses pulled the wooden sled through the corn field as we snapped off the dried ears of corn. When the wagon and sled were full, they were driven to the barn to be unloaded. We kept working filling white oak baskets we had bought from the Cheraw Indians for two bits each, dumping them into the wagon and sled when they returned. When we had picked all the corn, we shucked it and tossed the ears into the corn crib, saving the shucks for fodder. We estimated that we had grown the equivalent of one hundred bushels of shelled corn. Sean set about milling two large barrels into cornmeal for our own food. The rest of us scythed down the stalks and stacked them into shocks to dry for a few days. Once they were completely dry, we stored them in the loft.

The Irish and sweet potatoes were ready to dig. We hitched the horses to the breaking plow and turned them up to the top of the ground. They were cleaned and left to dry before we stacked them in crates. Immature or damaged potatoes were kept for hog feed. The best were chosen for seed potatoes and stored separately in the rock-lined cellar near the house in oat straw. The rest were for our winter food and were added to the cabbages, turnips, pumpkins, and dried onions tied up in braids in the cellar. The cellar had a heavy locust door that fit tightly with metal hinges and latches to keep critters from raiding the cellar.

Tobacco harvest came next. We hired some of Red Hat's men to help us at this point. The whole plant was cut down with cane knives, and the stalks split down the middle and laid in the wagon. We threaded the split plants on oak withes and hung them in the rafters to cure. The oxen dragged a large maple stump into the barn, where it was kept smoldering on the dirt floor. Sometimes we would add fruit wood like apple when we had it, but not hickory or most other woods as they would give the tobacco a harsh taste.

The last harvest was the indigo. All the foliage was cut from the woody stalks and larger branches. It smelled bad when freshly cut. It was placed in the large kettles and fresh water was poured over it until it was just submerged. A piece of dense wood like locust was placed on top to keep the foliage under water. In eighteen hours, the quick fermentation of the indigo caused the water to bubble like it was boiling. The water turned a dark violet. The water from the vats was poured into other kettles and slowly simmered until nothing but a purple mash was left in the bottom, which was collected and set aside to add to the rest later. The fermented foliage was simmered and stirred and pounded until all the seeds and leaf matter settled to the bottom. The smell was horrible. It would make a skunk throw up his lunch. We could hardly stand it. We wore rags over our faces with rosemary or other herbs to mask the smell. It smelled like rotting flesh and decayed vegetation. Local lore said that the smell was fatal to Negroes, so only whites or Indians were allowed to work with it. Once it had simmered down to a thick mash, it was spread onto trays to dry in layers two inches thick. After it was completely dry, it was cut into blocks about three by six inches. Then it was carefully weighed and packed in our best barrels. The weight and plantation of origin was burned into the top of the barrel. This year's crop would fill only a modest sized keg, but it was worth a small fortune.

The tobacco was weighed and packed in barrels with the type and weight burned into the top of the barrels. Our three barrels of tobacco and one of indigo were hauled down to Cheraw Landing and sent downriver to Georgetown. We saved enough unprocessed indigo and tobacco seed for next year's crop, plus two more acres of each. Due to the value of the crop, I went to Georgetown with Keenan, Mark, Sean and Logan for company. We were all armed with rifles, pistols and cutlasses. We took Mrs. Quick's crop and Mrs. Harrington's crop to market with us. We used one of the company scows with a trusted crew. As an added precaution, six swivel guns had been mounted on the scow.

The trip down the river was pleasant and uneventful. It was nice to be back in a town again! We all went for haircuts and shaves. The boys came by the shipping office to draw their wages. They spent some of it for new clothes and sundries, but held on to most of it. I took the other boys' pay back with me. We went over the books. The sale of the indigo and tobacco had paid the expenses and cleared a small profit! The seven hands would receive five Spanish dollars each. My share was $350, and the company's was $175. It was a good beginning.

While we were there, *Banshee* came into port. It was so good to see old shipmates again. Edward arranged a dinner for all of us that night. There was a lot of story telling going on way into the night. *Banshee* would carry our goods across the sea. It was a happy coincidence.

Our trip back upriver was aided by a friendly breeze. We were free of the responsibility of our cargo, we had money in our pockets, and it was a fine day. We made it to the landing before dark and unloaded the extra kettles, flour, salt, sugar and tea we had brought with us. We then took the ferry across to Cheraw. I treated the boys to a fine dinner at the hotel where we were staying. None of them had ever stayed anywhere so nice.

The next morning we paid a visit to the Bank of Cheraw where I deposited most of my money and helped the boys open accounts of their own. I opened accounts for the three younger ones, too, taking the liberty of depositing most of their money in their new accounts. None had ever had a bank account before this. They were amazed when I explained that the bank would pay them to keep their money for them! Our trip home was a happy one. Our first year in the wilderness had been a success.

Upon returning home, we told Priscella of our trip, the unexpected visitors from *Banshee,* and our modest profit. She was pleased, but her mind seemed elsewhere. She fed us a wonderful supper of ham, sweet potatoes, applesauce and cornbread. After the boys were settled, we stayed up talking by the fireplace. She seemed to want to talk, but was having a difficult time getting around to it.

"What is it Priscella? Are ye homesick for Ireland?"

"No, Thomas, darling. My home is here with you. I love our life here together."

"Is something wrong?"

"No. Everything is right, very right."

A glow came over her. "Thomas, in late May we will have a wee bairn of our own!"

I felt a wave of emotion wash over me. I flushed with excitement. I was to be a father!

I pulled her to me and held her tightly in front of the dying embers of the fire. Hot tears of joy streamed down my face onto her shoulder. I stroked her face and felt tears upon it, too. We held each other in quietness, feeling the love and joy swirling around us. All of the successes of which I was so proud, paled in comparison to my love for Priscella and our unborn child.

THE WHEAT AND OATS
we had sown in the fall had come up nicely with
the mild winter rains. We cleared another two acre
strip beside the existing dormant indigo stalks and
got it ready for planting in the spring. We also added
another two acres for tobacco, and had it ready for
transplanting. We would rotate the corn, wheat, oats,
potato and tobacco locations each year. Planting
in the same place each year seemed to encourage
disease. The indigo would grow in the same place for
many years. This would give us a total of eighteen
acres under cultivation. In Ireland, this would have
been a respectable small farm for one of my father's
tenants, but it was far below our ultimate goals. Our
limit was labor. It took lots of labor to clear, plow
and plant the land, especially the tobacco and indigo
which required so much hand work. I did not want
to hire full-time help more than we already had, nor

did I have the money or inclination to buy slaves. Slavery was something my family had never approved, although it was very common in the lowland parts of the Carolinas and Georgia.

As we continued to clear land, we stacked the marketable timber along the creek to sell later. We expanded and moved the rail fences to accommodate the larger fields.

In January 1751, we rode along the banks of Phill's Creek until we reached the Pee Dee. The junction would be a suitable place for building a log raft assembly area. After some preliminary checking, I found it was not claimed by anyone. I made a trip to Cheraw and filed a claim for twenty acres, with about ten acres on each side of the creek where it joined the river. The high end of the north half was above the flood zone. I had Keenan, Logan and Sean build a rough ten foot by twenty foot square cabin with no windows and a small fireplace. It would be a temporary shelter while the log raft was being assembled.

We floated down the eight largest and longest logs. Logan and Sean fastened them together with lengths of heavy chain attached to the logs with large spikes. They left the last link unfastened. The unfastened ends were chained to large trees on the bank. The boom was out of the main river current. Once this log boom was in place, we floated down the other logs in a steady stream, one after another. The boys at the assembly end used logging pikes to direct incoming logs into an orderly fashion. Before we launched them, each log had been marked with a large "T." After a few days all the logs had been floated downstream and formed into a raft. A company scow came to what we were calling Turner's Landing. Once the scow was present, we closed the open end of the raft and let the scow guide the raft downstream to the Turner spar, mast and timber yard.

Floating down with the logs in the scow, we delivered 232 quality pine and hardwood logs. We received $600 for our efforts. The boys each got $7. I received just less than $400, and the company near $200. We took the scow back to Turner's Landing, which had a decent place to dock a few scows in the deeper end of the creek. Retracing our steps back home, I sent the money to the Bank of Cheraw the next time I went to town. I had also collected the boys' accumulated wages and delivered the money to them. They wanted to bank most of it, too.

The fall had been so mild that we had not butchered our hogs. In late January, we butchered twelve young hogs of about two hundred pounds each. Zachary and Logan were in charge. The hogs were humanely killed, hung up and bled. We collected the blood for fertilizer. Some of our neighbors made blood sausage, but none of us would eat it. We used our large kettles filled with boiling water to scald the hogs to make the hair slip. That would make the hides easier to scrape free of hair. With one well-placed blow to the pelvis and deft sawing down the carcass, they were neatly split into half-sides. A butcher table was set up to divide the carcasses into hams, shoulders, loins and bacon. The precious fat was tossed into other kettles where it was slowly rendered into lard. Artie skimmed off the foam that floated to the top. When it was purified, it was poured into small kegs. The remains from the rendering were collected and fried into cracklings, a special treat. The meat was packed into salt to draw out any blood and moisture. Then the pork was hung in the smoke house for several weeks over a slowly smoking fire of hickory wood. The trimmings from the carcass and head were mixed with lard, seasoned, and poured into crocks kept in the smoke house. We called it head cheese, and it was better than it sounded. The feet were smoked and kept for snacks.

We planned to sell the other twelve hogs, and sell the male lambs and keep the ewe lambs. Our one heifer calf was added to the herd, and the two steers were fattened. We hauled the hogs and sheep to Cheraw to sell.

In February 1751 began one of the longest periods of cold snowy weather ever seen in Marlboro County. The temperature stayed below freezing for five days. Phill's Creek had a thin layer of ice all along the edges of the flowing water. The water troughs froze, so we had to dump out the ice and refill the troughs each day with well water. We kept the animals in their stalls with extra feed and hay. The wind had been out of the northeast, and it brought huge fat snowflakes in swirling abundance. It was about ten inches deep on the level ground, but where the wind had drifted it, the snow was often over waist deep. Once we were through with our extra weather related chores each day, we had some fun with the unexpected mounds of snow. The boys had some snowball fights of historic proportions, lasting for hours. Snow forts appeared near the out buildings, with piles of snowball ammunition stacked at hand.

We had thought about hunting, as it would be easy to track in the snow, but it was too difficult to walk very far. We had been hearing wolves howling at night, and even during the day. The snow did not seem to impede their hunting.

On the morning of the fifth day, as the boys were doing their chores, Dylan came running to tell me he had seen a pack of several wolves along the edge of the creek. Dylan and I grabbed the rifles which we kept loaded by the door, and quickly primed the pans. As we bounded off the porch, the other boys all came at a dead run. The wolves had trotted into the clearing around the barn, and were clawing at the barn door. I passed a gun to each of the boys. As we rounded the corner of the house, a cold hand clasped my heart. Five wolves were in front of the barn, growling as they tried to dig under the heavy door. They were so preoccupied, that they failed to notice us only 30 yards away. I gave a hand signal to the boys to spread out. I held up one finger and pointed at myself and then at them. They seemed to understand. The wolves only lacked a few inches more of digging to be among our defenseless livestock inside the barn. My chest was tight, and my mouth was dry. I raised my gun and took careful aim. Looking to my left, I saw that the boys had done the same. I held my breath and squeezed the trigger. As soon as I fired, the others had all fired, too. As the powder smoke drifted away, we could see four wolves dead in front of the barn. A fifth was wounded and crawling away. Keenan ran after it and killed it with the butt of his rifle.

He turned to smile at his valor, but his face changed to horror.

"Dylan! Behind you!"

Dylan turned just as a previously unseen wolf pounced on him. The great grey wolf was instantly on him, shaking him like a rag doll. I had a still unfired second barrel on my rifle, but could not shoot for fear of hitting Dylan. Zachary, all of thirteen, grabbed an axe left where he had been splitting wood and ran straight at the wolf. He hit the wolf a wicked slash across the shoulders. It yelped and jumped aside. Quick as a flash it lurched for Zachary's throat. Just as it sprang, Zachary hit it with a crashing blow in the side of the head with the butt of the axe, snapping its neck. It sprawled in the blood stained snow as we ran to check on Dylan.

Before we reached him, we heard Priscella scream from the porch followed instantly by the roar of a gun. I ran to the house, finding a wolf dead at the door. The large gray wolf had raised up on his hind legs against the front door, pushing it open. Priscella had screamed while Artie, who had already grabbed a gun loaded with buckshot, fired from the great room. His shot had hit the wolf squarely in the chest from mere feet away. I comforted Priscella, told Artie to bolt the door, and ran back to Dylan. He was sitting up in the snow, holding his left arm. We eased his heavy coat off to see his arm hanging at an odd angle. I had Mark and Logan walk him to the house. I turned to check on Zachary. He was standing stooped over near the dead wolf. He was white as a sheet and shaking all over.

"Zach, you did well today. You're a very brave thirteen year old!"

When I got back to the house, I found Priscella pouring hot water on the blood stain on the floor of the dog-trot in front of the door. One of the boys had dragged the wolf off the porch behind the house. Mark had already cut Dylan's shirt away. It appeared that both bones were broken in his left forearm about mid-way to the elbow. I had a bottle of good Irish whisky tucked away for such occasions. I poured about three ounces in a mug of hot water with sugar added to it and had Dylan swill it down in several big gulps. Sean held him by the shoulders, and Mark held his arm just above and below the elbow. I grasped his wrist firmly and pulled. The broken bones snapped neatly back in place. Keenan handed me some slats from a potato crate. I laid one on top and another on the bottom of his forearm and held them there as Priscella quickly secured them in place with some lengths of torn cotton cloth. Mark fixed a sling for him. Dylan never cried out, but had tears of pain and fear rolling down his face. I had checked him over carefully. His heavy clothes had protected him from puncture wounds from the wolf's fangs.

"Well, Dylan, that wolf sure tried to eat you. I guess he would have, too, if you weren't such a thick skinned Irishman! And he ruined a good coat and shirt, too. Don't worry. I'll get some new things and take it out of your pay."

I couldn't keep a straight face as all the boys started laughing. Dylan smiled, but his skinny 11 year old body had been through a lot. We fixed him a pallet in the great room where Priscella could watch him during the day, and Zach made a pallet next to him at night.

"Artie, where did ye learn to shoot like that?"

"I don't know, your honor. But I'm glad I did!"

The other boys took all seven carcasses to the wood shop where they skinned the wolves and sewed over the worst holes. They salted the hides and tacked them up inside the shop. Later, they crafted them into seven wolf-skin hats. They had the face and ears showing on the front. The leg skins hung down from in front and behind their shoulders, with the thick pelt over their necks, and the tail hanging down their backs. They were well-made and lasted for years. They wore them with pride anytime the weather was the least bit cold. The sight of the boys with their seven hats earned them the name of Gray Wolf Boys from our Cheraw Indian neighbors. The name stuck, and over time, the plantation was commonly called Gray Wolf Plantation.

In the remaining days of winter, Keenan and Sean set about making barrels for our use. They had learned well. Keenan did the cooperage and Sean the hoops. Their barrels were good enough that some of the neighbors wanted to buy any surplus.

The boys sold several and kept half the proceeds for themselves, as they were working on company time and with company tools. They were pleased with the agreement, and regularly sent their extra savings to the bank at Cheraw.

The others were kept busy clearing eight more acres for crops: two each for tobacco and indigo, and four for corn, wheat and oats. Priscella convinced them to clear about a forty foot wide strip the length of the garden so she could plant more fruit trees. After some negotiation, it was decided the stumps could be left in the strip. Logan laid off the rows in the garden so Priscella and the younger boys could get the early crops of cabbage, onions, and greens started. Dylan was healed enough now to return to light work.

Father had sent word through Edward that a store would be a good idea. He added that he liked the idea of us hauling and shipping the neighbors produce, as it would be certain to be carried to market on Turner ships. He would be sending money for another wagon and team of oxen, as well as basic supplies for the store. I decided it would be best for Mark to be in charge of the store, freeing him from some of his other chores, except starting the indigo and tobacco. He would have an office in the store where he would keep our plantation books. He was excited about the opportunity.

We laid a rock foundation of sixteen feet by twenty feet, with a long front porch. It was built with nicely squared and fitted logs. There was a small fireplace in the south end. The windows were made of sturdy wood which locked from the inside, and a solid door which was secured with a heavy hasp and store-bought lock and key.

We had the indigo and tobacco transplanted and the corn

just coming up by late April. The ewes had lambed and the hogs had farrowed. The cows had calved, having one especially nice heifer and two bull calves.

Just before we were ready to start cutting the oats, word arrived to expect a shipment from Georgetown. We hitched the oxen to the wagon, and rode the horse to Cheraw Landing on the appointed date. Edward and Paul were there when we arrived. Their men had already unloaded the scow and had assembled a large wagon and two fine female oxen, complete with yokes and tack. They had sent goods to stock the store which we loaded in the two wagons. The store was to be the provision house for our plantation and to sell to the public. There were two kegs of nails, bars of iron and lead, two small kegs of gunpowder and a small box of musket repair tools. Sean had become proficient in repairs of that type. There were farm and hand tools, chain and rope. There were pots, pans, kitchen utensils, needles and thread, plus several bolts of cotton, wool, and linen cloth in various colors. There were a half-dozen rifled muskets and two shotguns. There was powdered ink, paper, beeswax candles, barrels of salt, boxes of tea, sacks of unroasted coffee beans, a barrel of sugar, two wheels of cheese, and a box of assorted spices.

Mark carefully arranged everything on shelves, and noted in his ledger books the prices for everything. He set up a desk by the window nearest the fireplace. He seemed proud of the extra responsibility we gave him. His self-confidence grew daily. It seems there was no job that he was given that he could not do, and do well. There was a bell mounted on the porch to ring if no he was away from the store attending to his other duties. I increased his pay to five shillings a week, plus his usual profit share.

He had taught the others to save the soiled bedding from the stalls for fertilizer and spread it on which ever fields were dormant. In the spring each year it was turned under before planting that field. The indigo plants had not been hurt by the cold. The temperatures had not gone low enough to damage them, and the snow on the ground had insulated the roots.

On a warm May morning, Artie rushed to find me as I was scything oats.

"Sir, Miss Priscella said to tell ye the child is coming soon, to please have your honor come as soon as you can, and to send for Mrs. Quick!"

I had Dylan hitch the horses to the wagon and fetch Mrs. Quick. I ran to the cabin to find Priscella propped up in bed with two kettles of water boiling by the fireplace.

"Husband, my time is near. My water broke this half hour and more. The pains are coming closer together and stronger each time. I do not think it will be long. This is one of those times I sorely miss my mother! Is Mrs. Quick on her way?"

"Aye, my love. What can I do?"

"Stay close by me and help me to be brave."

We heard the clatter of hooves and the wagon at the front porch. Mrs. Quick let herself in the room.

"Thomas, you will soon be a father. Please fetch me two clean wash basins, a large pitcher of hot water, and some soap and clean towels."

She rolled up her sleeves, put a clean smock over her clothes, and washed her hands. She positioned Priscella just so in the bed. She tied stout cotton cords to the footboards of the bed, and placed one in both of Priscella's hands. Her feet were wedged against the footboard. I supported Priscella's head and shoulders. Each time she had a pain she was to push against the footboard and pull against the cords.

Mrs. Quick could see the top of the baby's head. With the next pain, she gave a mighty push and the child was born. Mrs. Quick cleaned its tiny nose and mouth, and holding it up by its ankles gave it a sharp swat on the bottom. The baby immediately gave a lusty cry. As she was wrapping it in a towel, I saw it urinate all over Mrs. Quick, so I knew it was a boy! She handed him to Priscella. He had wisps of red hair. I kissed Priscella gently on the forehead. The baby quickly found his first meal and was happily rooting and grunting. We named him Thomas, Jr. He would grow to be the apple of our eyes and make us very proud in the years to come. For now my heart was swollen with love for my tiny son and my dear wife. I offered a silent prayer for God to bless and keep them both.

The store was proving successful. The neighbors in the area, including Red Hat's village, found it convenient to buy from us. They liked the idea of us shipping their produce to market for them, and our plantation would be the collecting point. We ordered two more large wagons for the fall. We planned to buy two more pairs of oxen from Mr. Grant.

As late summer gave way to fall, we sowed four acres each to wheat and oats, doubling our previous planting. We would need the extra feed for the additional animals, and would sell the excess in the store. Once the grain had been sown, we started the corn harvest. Our corn cribs were almost full. We set a couple of the boys to milling corn meal for ourselves and some to sell. They also custom milled corn for the neighbors for a small fee. If they didn't have their own kegs or small barrels, we were happy to sell them some.

The tobacco crop was good. It filled much more of the curing barn than it had the year before. The slowly smoking fires on the dirt floors scented the air all day and night. It became a smell I pleasantly associated with autumn and harvest time.

The indigo crop did not appear to have been hurt by the cold weather. We had been lucky. Had the temperature dipped lower we could have lost the plants all the way back to the root, or even worse, lost them completely. The extra kettles were sure handy. The putrid work was done none too soon. We barreled about $700 worth of indigo.

Finally, the Irish and sweet potatoes were dug and stored in the cellar along with the cabbage, carrots, pumpkins, onions, and other garden produce that would store well. As the neighbors had not yet finished processing their indigo, and the weather was cool, we did our fall butchering.

Of the pigs, sheep and steers, we kept what we needed and sent the others to market in Cheraw.

When we were finished, I sent the boys with the wagons to the neighbors to pick up their indigo and tobacco. They would pay us a fee for hauling it to market. We had successfully begun our freight business. They also gave us lists of things they need from Georgetown that we would buy for them and deliver for a small profit. They seemed happy with the arrangement as we were.

The trip down river was uneventful. But there were stories of scows being attacked and their cargos stolen. The indigo and tobacco sold well and returned a profit for all of us. Hauling the neighbors' goods added some to the profit. This year ended well, and saw our work in the wilderness growing and prospering. We had found joy and freedom in our new home, and had come to treasure it.

9

THE EARLY MONTHS OF 1752 were cold and wet. The only thing on the place that seemed to be enjoying it was the wheat and oats. They were thick, tall, and green. The rest of us were wet, miserable, and tired of the mud and rain. Travel along the road was difficult. On days when it wasn't raining too much, but was too wet to cut timber, the boys went hunting. They often brought back a fat turkey or a deer. Any of the venison that we didn't eat after a few days was salted, smoked and dried into jerky. We often shared a hind-quarter of meat with Mrs. Harrington or Mrs. Quick.

On days when the weather would allow the boys cleared timber. They got a total of four acres cleared and the stumps pulled. When things dried enough, they used the breaking plow and harrow. Two acres were adjacent to the indigo field to expand our planting, and two were destined for tobacco. We now had eight oxen. When all eight were hitched and pulling, the stumps popped right out of the soft ground. The rail fences around the cultivated ground were expanded to surround the new fields.

Just as the fields were finished, Mark fell ill. A customer at the store from Mrs. Harrington's plantation had been in to buy some patent medicine for fever. He had said there was fever at the plantation. Three days later, Mark began to have a severe headache, body aches, a horrible cough and high fever.

We fixed a bed for him in the store to try to keep him out of the house, exposing the rest of us, especially little Thomas. I checked on him all through the night and the next day, and brought him water mixed with a little whisky and honey. I kept the fire going for him. He was even worse the next day. Priscella peeled the bark from willow branches and made a tea with a little sugar. This lessened his fever, and we continued the whisky toddies. He didn't feel like eating much, but I took him soup and oatmeal. I wouldn't allow Priscella near him. On the third day of his illness, Sean and Logan, who had helped in tending him, fell ill. We moved them into the store, too. They received the same care Mark had gotten. He was finally some better, but not well enough to be up and out. At least he was eating and drinking, and the fever had left him. Because I had been tending them, I stayed in the store, too.

As I had feared, three days after the Perkins boys fell ill, I was stricken, too. I felt its full wrath. The fever would rise until I poured sweat, soaking the bedding. Then it would plunge, setting in with a shaking chill. My head felt like I had been hit with a hammer. Every muscle in my body hurt as if I had been beaten. I was able to take some of the willow bark tea which helped a little, as did the whisky toddies. Logan and Sean were slowly improving. Mark was well enough that he took over caring for us. Priscella would leave baskets for us at the door, knock, and walk away. It was hard being away from her. In my fevered thoughts, I wondered what would become of her and young Thomas if the fever took me, as it had the man at Mrs. Harrington's. I made Mark promise that if I died of the fever, that he would get them down to Georgetown to my brother, Edward.

I gradually got better, and knew I would not die. But Mrs. Harrington had cared personally for the man who had died. She had fallen ill and died a few days later. She had been buried beside her husband in their family cemetery, as had their hired man. None of the rest of our group had fallen ill.

Mrs. Harrington's daughter came from Charleston after the news arrived. We expressed our condolences and offered to help. She indicated she had no desire to keep the plantation and offered to sell it to us.

The plantation had a good house, much like ours. There was a good barn, tobacco barn and out buildings. There were forty acres in cultivation, of which ten were well established indigo. The others were in a rotation of tobacco, corn, wheat, oats, and potatoes. Additionally, there was a two acre garden and a nice fruit orchard. The balance of the plantation was timbered, except for a forty acre pasture where the pines had been removed. The perimeter was fenced, and the garden and cropland had a good fence around it. Her land lay across Phill's Creek from us on the same side of the road. Her daughter wanted to keep only a few items of personal significance, and let the remainder go with the property, including all the farm implements and livestock.

There was a complicating factor. Mrs. Harrington had a family of slaves who had worked her land. The father was a man in his mid-thirties named Jimmy Harrington. His wife was named Charlotte and a teenaged son named Jack. Mrs. Harrington's daughter insisted they sell with the property. She asked $600 for Jimmy, $400 for Charlotte, and $300 for Jack. If we did not buy them, she would take them to the slave market in Charleston. Jimmy pleaded with me to keep his family together.

This brought the total to $2180, to which I agreed. The next morning, Dylan hitched the fine draft horses I had bought with the farm to the wagon, and we headed to Cheraw. The lawyer met us at the bank and drew up the legal documents for the land and the slaves. I went to the Cheraw District Clerk's office and filed the deed for the land and the bill of sale on the slaves and livestock. It struck me as wrong that the same document that transferred horses and oxen transferred the lives of humans.

I asked Mark if he would move into the Harrington house as overseer for her plantation, plus continue his responsibilities with the store and as plantation clerk. I offered him a good raise. Although it was a big responsibility for a nineteen year old, he readily accepted.

"Mark, I believe your parents would be very proud of you."

"I think they would be, too, Thomas. Thank you for your confidence in me." He said with a moist gleam in his eyes.

Sean, Logan, and Arthur, who were nineteen, eighteen, and thirteen, would move over there with him. The three of them were very close and would not consider living apart. Charlotte would take care of the house and the garden. The servants had a tidy cabin near the tobacco barn and their own half-acre garden.

I talked to Jimmy and his family about an idea I had. I would free them as slaves and sign them on as indentured servants until their debt was repaid. They sat awe-stricken, but nodded agreement.

"Mr. Turner, sah, me and my family never figured they was no way we'd ever gets to be free. This is a mighty good thing. We'll works extra hard for you, sah."

"It looks like we have a deal then, Jimmy."

We shook hands on our agreement. I felt better about it. I had never intended to have slaves, but had felt obligated to buy them. Perhaps this would be a good opportunity for all of us. Mark wrote down the whole agreement, so that if something happened to me, the deal would be binding.

Our plantation now consisted of seven hundred and three acres, including Turner's Landing. We had sixty acres in cultivation, with fourteen acres in established indigo, several oxen and a good bull, two milk cows, two fine matched draft horses, two general purpose horses, ten sows and two boars, lots of sheep and even more chickens. We had five stout wagons, two fine cabins, excellent outbuildings, a mill, a store, and a smith and carpenter shop. The whole place was called the Turner Plantation, but was divided into the Harrington Farm and the Gray Wolf Farm. As our land was now on both sides of Phill's Creek, and it had grown into a small community, it came to be known as Turner's Crossing.

Mark trained Jack to assist him with his responsibilities as a horticulturist. He was smart and a fast learner. Mark also taught him his letters and numbers, and soon taught him to read and write. The corn and potatoes were planted on both farms. With the extra help of the three servants, we were able to handle the additional acres. The tedious process of transplanting the new acres of indigo and tobacco went smoothly with three experienced workers helping.

Our cow oxen and milk cows calved, and the ewes lambed. The oats were cut and thrashed, followed by the wheat. The straw was stored in the lofts, and the grain barreled and stored. We milled a few barrels of wheat flour, and milled a good bit for the neighbors.

Once the crops were laid by, we started the process of sending logs downstream. When the company scow came up river to the landing, it brought kegs of sugar, salt, nails and tea. There were also many bolts of various types of cloth, farm tools, house wares, and a couple of large rounds of cheese. They brought barrels of turpentine and pine tar. These would serve our own needs and restock the store. It also brought a letter from Father.

My son, Thomas, I pray that this finds ye well. You seem to be a man of business. Your brothers and I fully support your decision to buy the other plantation. We have been proud of the way you have handled your plantation and have managed to return a good profit to the company and yourself. I regret to tell you that your mother passed away of a fever in February. I miss her greatly. I am proud of you and would love to see you and to meet Thomas, Jr.

Your father,
Josiah Turner

I was saddened by the unexpected loss of my mother. She

had been a wonderful mother to all of us. It made me remember how far our new home was from the land of our birth. Zachary's and Dylan's parents also sent letters. It occurred to me that only Keenan and Mark could read and write. I determined that the others would be educated soon. I discussed the idea with Priscella who thought it to be a good thing, but indicated that she would have no time to do it herself. There was an educated young English girl who worked in Mrs. Quick's house who might be a good teacher. Her name was Ashley Smith. She was about 18 and was a second cousin of Mrs. Quick who had come to live with her after her parents died. We decided Priscella would speak to Mrs. Quick and Ashley soon.

Priscella thought it would be an especially good idea to have someone else take care of the teaching, as she would be busier than usual around April next spring with our new baby. I was tremendously happy, and remembered just how much I loved Priscella and Thomas. He had grown to be an adventurous little tyke, who never met a ladder he couldn't climb. He loved to sit on my lap while I told him stories. One of his favorites was the story of the wolf attack. "Bad wooffs!" he would say, then growl.

Mrs. Quick agreed to let Ashley teach the boys after supper when her chores were finished. We ordered some slates and primers. She began her work soon. Mrs. Quick had specified that Ashley not teach the Negroes. We would abide by her wishes, but Mark continued to teach Jack, who was learning rapidly. He, in turn, was teaching his parents. They were very discreet as many people did not support educating slaves.

We had noticed Mark was coming to our house each night when Ashley taught the other boys. He would bring his account books and work on them on the table in the great room where the others were being taught. After the lessons, he volunteered to walk her home each night. Priscella and I smiled to each other, for we saw young love budding. Soon, Mark asked Mrs. Quick if he could call on Ashley. She willingly agreed.

As the summer progressed, we set the hands to clearing another two acres next to the indigo, two more for corn, and another two for tobacco. The draft horses pulled the logs to the creek, and the oxen pulled the stumps and piled them in the edge of the woods. We used the draft horses to pull the breaking plow, and the lighter horses to pull the harrow. The horses could cover more ground in a day than the oxen

One evening after Mark and I reviewed the accounts, he asked my blessing to marry Ashley in January. He was mature and financially able to take a wife. I agreed.

"You've grown into a fine responsible young man. I am proud of you and happy for you."

As he left, he turned back. "I do wish that my family was alive to be here."

He asked Mrs. Quick the next day. She gave her blessing. They posted their banns at the store as there was no church yet.

Harvest progressed well, and yields were good. Once the indigo was processed and the tobacco cured, we gathered the neighbors' produce for shipping to Georgetown. It took all five wagons and our ten pair of oxen to haul it all to Cheraw Landing. We filled two scows for the trip. Prices were good. The fall butchering was soon finished and the surplus animals marketed. The year of 1752 had been a good one for us.

10

THERE WAS NOT A Presbyterian minister in the entire Cheraw three county district. An Anglican minister resided in Cheraw, but he would marry only Anglicans. There was a Methodist minister who rode a circuit in the district. He was scheduled to be in Brightsville on the third Sunday in January. He could do the wedding service the preceding day. That would not leave much time.

Mrs. Quick had a wedding dress her daughter had worn. She and Priscella started to fit it for Ashley. Mark rode to Cheraw to get a marriage license. A few invitations were sent around to the neighbors. It would be a ten o'clock wedding, to be followed by a banquet at Mrs. Quick's house. Mark asked Sean to stand up with him. Ashley was close to the Grant's daughter, Constance. She asked her to stand up with her. There was no one to give the bride away. Ashley asked me if I would take the place of her deceased father. I was honored to oblige.

The boys set about the Harrington house to make it suitable for the new woman in our extended family. The walls in the bedroom were cleaned and rubbed down with turpentine and linseed oil. The old stuffing was removed from the pillows and mattress and replaced with cotton we had bought in Georgetown. The hearth was scrubbed, and the kitchen walls cleaned and rubbed down. The boys even moved the outhouse to a new site, set over a freshly dug hole, and the old one filled.

On the night before the wedding Reverend Browning arrived at our cabin. We tended his horse and put him in a good stall with fresh bedding. We fixed a nice dinner for the minister that night. He was given one of the empty bedrooms. The Perkins boys moved out of the Harrington house for a while, and moved back in with us.

We were up early the next morning getting cleaned up and dressed for the wedding. We loaded into the wagon with the matched draft horses for the short drive to Quick plantation. Dylan had braided ribbons in their manes and harnesses.

When we got to the wedding, we found a good crowd of neighbors assembled there. The chairs and benches in the great room were arranged facing the windows. The Reverend Browning moved to the front of the room accompanied by Mark and Sean. Constance appeared at the minister's side.

"All rise!"

Ashley was clutching my arm tightly as we moved to the front. She was radiant. Mark was beaming.

"Who gives this woman's hand in marriage?"

"I do, sir."

The ceremony proceeded without complication. The matrimonial knot was firmly tied. The tables were heavily laden with good food. There was roast venison loin, a cured ham, a finely roasted turkey, yeast rolls, sweet potatoes, carrots cooked in butter, beautiful layer cakes and pumpkin pies. Sweet and hard cider were both available, along with Irish whisky and rum punch.

When the banquet was over, Dylan loaded Mark and Ashley in the decorated wagon, along with Ashley's trunk. As they left, they were showered with rice. Dylan drove them to the Harrington house which would be theirs alone for a week. I arranged for Charlotte to leave a basket with a day's worth of food on the front porch each day, and to retrieve the dirty dishes from the previous day.

Dylan returned to the Quick plantation to bring the rest of us home. The minister rode with us to the house to retrieve his horse for his trip to Brightsville. Before he left, he asked us to think about building a church house that could be shared by all the people in the area. His suggestion caught our attention. In the following days I discussed it with the neighbors. The Grants were Methodists, the Smiths were Anglican. Both Irby families were Presbyterians like us. Mrs. Quick was an Anglican. She agreed to donate two acres across from our store for a church and a school.

Within days, construction was beginning. The two acres were heavily wooded. The trees were removed to use in building the school and church. Certain large trees were left on the lots. The foundations were laid out, and chestnut trees were used for the sleepers, and yellow poplar for the puncheons. Stone fireplaces were built for both. Squared and fitted pine logs were used to raise the walls. The rafters were made of sawed pine.

Keenan had a pile of cured oak shingles sufficient for both roofs. He had cured poplar boards he used to build the doors, and Sean made heavy ornamental hinges for both. The windows would be shuttered only for now. Perhaps someone would donate glass windows later.

Nicely grained oak was used for benches and pews. The trimmed limbs were used to build a fence around the sides and back to connect into Mrs. Quick's fence.

The Methodist minister agreed to come once a quarter, as did the Anglican minister from Cheraw. As time went by, we all pretty much attended regardless of who was preaching. We knew all the same hymns. Sharing the church and school seemed to increase our sense of community. The church building came to be used as a public meeting hall.

Ashley did a good job with the school. Our five who had not been educated attended intermittently, as did the Grant, Irby and Smith children. There were about 11 children attending there some days, and rarely less than five. The fee to attend was one Spanish dollar per semester, and there was a spring, summer, and fall term. School dismissed during planting and harvesting seasons. Ashley taught reading, writing and simple arithmetic. She also taught history and geography. Our company donated supplies for the school.

Mrs. Quick approached me in the spring just before planting time was to begin with a proposal. She had no family left in the area. She was tired of running the plantation. She had a son in Georgetown who had asked her to move in with them. She asked if I would be interested in buying her plantation with all its buildings, livestock and slaves. Her plantation was four hundred acres, mostly forested. The boundaries were the creek on the south, the road on the east, and stone markers on the west and north. It was fenced all the way around, and the forty cultivated acres were fenced to keep the livestock out. Of the forty acres, ten were established indigo. She had an excellent house, a large barn, tobacco barn, and other out buildings. She had a good wagon, a pair of draft horses, a pair of cow oxen, a milk cow, a flock of sheep and several chickens. The slaves consisted of one family, with the father, Nathan, and his wife, Betty. She kept the house and garden, and was gifted in sewing and working wool. They had a teenage daughter named Esther who worked in the fields and the house. Mrs. Quick said she was becoming a good cook and made excellent cheeses.

We discussed the price and terms. She first specified that the old milk cow, named Nora Jane, be allowed to stay on the plantation until she died. She had become a pet to her. She specified that the slaves be priced at half the going price to give them a head start on buying their freedom. I agreed easily to those terms, and we settled on a total price of $1640. She wanted her silver, dishes and a special quilt. The rest of the furniture and kitchen items were to be left behind. It was an excellent buy for us. We would miss her company and wisdom.

"Thomas, dear friend, ye look sad. I am sixty-two years old and healthy. I have had a good life here, but I am alone now but for my friends like your family. The money from the sale will provide for me the rest of my life. I will be with my son and his family. Be glad rather than sad."

"You were our first friend here. You delivered young Thomas. We have grown to treasure your friendship. It is for ourselves we are sad. We wish you God's speed."

I went to the Cheraw District Clerk's office and filed the bill of sale on the livestock and slaves, and the deed on the property.

We had drawn up our own documents based on the Harrington documents. I had written Mrs. Quick a letter of credit that would be honored at our Georgetown shipping office.

When I returned, I offered Keenan the job as overseer at the Quick farm. He would continue his carpenter's work and live in Mrs. Quick's former home with Zachary and Dylan. I would double his wages and he would still be eligible for his profit share. He jumped at the opportunity.

He had developed the skills and maturity to handle the position. He had always been somewhat of a loner. He interacted well with all of us, but tended to keep his own council. He never spoke of his family he had left behind, and we respected his privacy. He worked hard and never shirked responsibility or cheated anyone.

I made the same offer to the Quick slaves I had made to the Harrington family, to become indentured servants. They gratefully agreed.

Our combined plantation was now one thousand one hundred and three acres. We had a store, a mill, a carpenter shop, a blacksmith, a freight business, a school and a church. We were roughly halfway between Cheraw and Brightsville. The name of Turner's Crossing was now in common usage. I was proud of what we had accomplished so far. We had carved a home out of the wilderness. Like a young tender plant, it was healthy and growing, but vulnerable. Could we keep growing? Could we keep what we had worked so hard to create? My pride was shaded by private, silent doubts.

The spring planting went smoothly. Although there were more acres to plant, we had more hands in the fields, more implements, and more draft horses and oxen. All of the oxen and milk cows calved. The sheep had a beautiful crop of spring lambs, the sows farrowed lots of squirming piglets, and there were yellow chicks following their mothers around the farmstead.

We soon noticed there was something peculiar about Mrs. Quick's pet cow, Nora Jane. Although her name may have been pretty, ugly went all the way to the bone. She was sway backed. One horn curved up and one curved down. Her tail had been broken at some time and had a forty-five degree curve to the right. She had a bad udder, which was damaged and dry in one quarter. Whenever she was milked, she rarely missed an opportunity to kick Dylan or knock over the bucket. If one was careless to get in front of her, she frequently used her upward horn to the seat of your pants. I had promised Mrs. Quick that Nora Jane would have a home on the farm as long as the cow lived, but I was determined that would not be too long. Dylan was tender hearted to all the animals. He interceded on her behalf, and she was allowed to stay.

Dylan had grown into a fine young man, too. He was kind and patient with the animals, but had no problems butchering them for food. He was honest and dependable, and both he and Zachary were like sons to us.

Not all was as frustrating as the old cow. On April 11, 1753, just after lunch, Priscella sent for Charlotte and Betty. I knew from the look on her face, it was time for the baby. They both arrived quickly, carrying things necessary for delivering the baby. Ashley Cunningham came from the school to help. I was sent to the kitchen to keep water boiling on the hearth. Her labor was shorter and easier than it had been with Thomas. She delivered a fine son we named James in honor of my brother. He was a fine strapping boy with red curly hair and pale blue eyes like his brother.

There was more work than we could get done by ourselves. We hired four men and two women from Red Hat's village. They asked two bits a day. They worked hard and were worth every penny I paid them.

The blackberry canes along the creek were thick with fat, ripe berries that summer. They were favorite treats of the younger boys who would proudly bring them to Priscella to be made into a cobbler to eat now and jelly to put on biscuits later. I think they ate more on the creek bank than they ever brought home. Zachary, Dylan and Artie set out with small pails to pick blackberries. They had been at it for some time when tragedy struck. A huge copperhead lay coiled in the shade of the canes. As Artie bent down to reach a low-hanging berry, the snake lunged at him, burying his fangs deep in his throat. He screamed in shock and agony. Before he could react, the snake bit him again in his face. Zach and Dylan ran to his side. Zach grabbed a sturdy branch and killed the snake. He stayed with Arthur, as Dylan ran for help. Artie writhed in agony, and called for his brothers with Zachary supporting his head in his lap. It was over in seconds, as the venom pulsed through his body.

"Thomas! Thomas! Come quick! Artie has been snake bit! Oh, sir, come now!"

A wagon was standing hitched at the barn. We jumped into the wagon and slapped the horses into a run for the creek. I had sent Mark to find Sean and Logan.

We stopped the wagon and climbed through the rail fence. Zachary could be heard crying softly. Artie was already dead. We laid his slender thirteen year old body in the back of the wagon and headed slowly to the house. His brothers arrived just as we drove up to the cabin. When they realized what had happened, a wave of anguish engulfed them, and swirled around all of us. We were in shock. Zachary could not speak of Artie's last moments. Sean and Logan were inconsolable. The three Perkins boys were orphans; each other was all they had. Now Artie was gone. It would be months before their grief eased. We would miss his laughter and stories. He was buried in the small cemetery on the Harrington plantation.

Harvest arrived with warm, dry, and bountiful days. We hauled our indigo and tobacco to Cheraw Landing along with the neighbors' produce. As piracy had been reported on the lower river, we were all armed. We had the scow fitted with four pounders in the bow and stern, and swivel guns along the sides.

The wind was kind to our lug sail, and the scow made a rapid trip with the oarsmen and the current. As we approached Snow Island where the Lynches River sluggishly merged into the Pee Dee, we saw two scows rowing hard to intercept us. If there was any doubt of their intention, it became clear as they were crowded with armed men. At two hundred yards they opened fire on us. From the erratic fall of their shots, it was likely they were firing smooth-bore muskets. We returned fire with our rifled muskets, which were much more accurate at that range. Logan hauled on the steering oar to bring the forward gun to bear on the nearest pirate scow. Sean expertly laid the gun to strike just below the water line. With a great bellow and eruption of flame and smoke, the forward gun blew a gaping hole in the scow. Water began to pour into the side. Although they rowed with all their might for the shore, the scow settled quickly into the swirling water of the Pee Dee fifty yards from shore. The would-be pirates were caught in the current and drowned. A few managed to struggle to the muddy banks of Snow Island.

The other scow, seeing our bow gun had fired and was not now loaded rowed hard and fast directly toward us. As Sean rushed to reload the forward gun, Logan swung the stern around to meet the challenge. The pirates poured musket balls into our scow. We sought shelter as best we could, returning their fire. Six of the swivels could be brought to bear, and at my signal, all spoke at once. Their combined three hundred musket balls at such short range brought death to our enemies. As the stern gun was laid and fired, it opened a huge hole in the side of the pirate scow. The steering oar was put over bringing the now reloaded bow gun into play. Sean again sent a solid iron ball deep into the side. River water rushed in and the scow sank in mid-stream. The few survivors drowned in the river, except two men who managed to make it to the island clinging to wreckage.

I was strongly tempted to pursue them on the island and hunt down the survivors to have them tried and hung in Georgetown. However, I could not risk such a valuable cargo to seek revenge. The pirates shook their fists and shouted obscenities at us from the shore of Snow Island. At one hundred and fifty yards, they were easy targets for our riflemen who dropped them with their curses still on their lips. The men whooped in triumph over the river pirates. As I reloaded my rifle, I noticed my hands were shaking.

That fall and winter, pirating on the Pee Dee almost completely stopped. The effectiveness of Turner Shipping and Trade in getting cargo safely to market did not go unnoticed. The year 1753 had been profitable, but bittersweet. We had gained baby James, and lost Arthur.

11

JANUARY 1754 ARRIVED
with sleet and cold rain. We all hurried about our
daily chores trying to get back inside where it was
warm and dry. Mark had taken one of the wagons and
our best draft horses to Cheraw to do some banking
for us. He had put the wagon tarp up on the hoops,
and had taken a heavy wool blanket to wrap around
him. He spent the night at the hotel and concluded
his business early the next day. He crossed over to
Cheraw Landing and picked up three barrels of flour,
two barrels of sugar, and a large box of wool blankets
to stock at the plantation store. The horses were fat
and in good condition for the drive. He had fitted
them with double-layered canvas blankets under
their harness. The blankets kept them from chilling
due to the freezing rain.

He was wearing a good warm coat, hat and
gloves, and the wool blanket. As the freezing rain

was blowing under the wagon tarp, he wrapped a spare tarp around him in an effort to keep dry. The road was muddy and had not frozen. The pulling was hard, but the team was up to the task. They knew warm stalls, feed and hay waited for them at home. They needed little encouragement to pull hard.

The freezing rain and sleet kept pelting them all the way home. The road conditions caused the trip to stretch out to a long, tough nine hours. When Mark pulled up in front of the store, he discovered he could not get off the wagon. The tarp he had wrapped around him had frozen solid! Dylan heard him drive up. He was amused by what he saw. He laughed until his sides hurt as he used a broom handle to free Mark from his icy shroud. We all had a good laugh at his expense.

A week later, he came by to let us know Ashley was expecting a baby in August. Of course we couldn't help from teasing him that we couldn't spare him from harvest in August, so not to waste any time about getting the baby delivered.

Keenan Harmon was now nineteen and a master carpenter, cooper and wheelwright. He did a good job as overseer for the Quick farm. Sean Perkins was twenty-one. He was an accomplished blacksmith, farrier and gunsmith. He could make almost anything from iron. His brother, Logan, was nineteen. He was a jack of all trades. He could assist with a level of skill with carpentry, smithing, milling, crops, animals and butchering. We relied on him heavily. Sean and Logan were as close as two brothers could be. Although they had their fights, woe be to him who came between them.

Zachary was a tall, strong seventeen years old. He could cook anything, and was responsible for curing the farms various meats. Now, he rarely heard from his parents, and only wrote them sporadically. He was close friends with Dylan Caswell, who was now fifteen. Dylan was a natural with animals. He was the plantation's herdsman. He could repair harness and tack, and did some outside work for the neighbors. He, too, rarely communicated with his family in Ireland. Both were fiercely independent and extremely loyal to our family. They considered themselves part of our family, as we did them.

Young Thomas was three and a half, and a busy active child. He especially loved Dylan, Zach and Ashley. His brother, James, was two. He gave us all a run for our money. Both boys loved to climb up in my lap while I read to them or told stories. I loved to take them with me when I was doing my chores or driving the wagon around the area. They were good little boys who really brightened our days.

None of us had been back to Ireland since we had left in 1749. Priscella and I talked about it for a while, and decided when the spring crops had been planted we would book passage back to Ireland on *Banshee*. Zach and Dylan still had parents living there. They would join us on the trip. My brothers, James, Edward, and William would go with us, too. We were excited and working on our plans. We would need to return in time for fall harvest. Mark would act as my deputy in my absence and remain in charge of the Harrington farm. Keenan would continue to function as overseer for the Quick farm, while Logan would be in charge at Gray Wolf Farm. We would need extra help from Red Hat's folks while we were away.

Even in our eagerness for our trip, the work of the plantation had to continue. Once the spring planting was done, we headed down river. We were to meet *Banshee* there.

When we arrived at Georgetown, I was delighted to find

that William was waiting for us. He had made it in from Jamaica the previous day, as had James from Charleston. They had caught passage on *Banshee* as she sailed through. Of course, Edward was there, too. It was the first time there had been four of us brothers together in years. While William had brought his daughters from Kingston, James' wife and children had decided to stay behind in Charleston.

A familiar gruff voice called out "Well look at ye now Thomas, with a beautiful wife and two fine bairn at your side! It is fine to see ye, lad."

"Well met, Brian! James, you and William remember our sailing master, Brian Clancy."

"Well met, Mr. Clancy."

"Thomas, could these two oak trees of young men be the bilge rats we set ashore with ye five years ago?"

"Hello, Mr. Clancy!" Zachary replied.

"Proud to see ye well, sir!" Dylan grinned.

"What do you feed these lads in the Carolinas? They are big as oxen and almost as smart!"

"Hold fast, shipmate. They both read and write and know their sums."

"Would ye lads like to make some extra money on the voyage as topmen?"

"Aye, sir! We would!"

The tide began to ebb at about nine in the morning. *Banshee* worked her way out under topsails and jibs sail alone until she reached the open sea.

"McNamara! Steer straight and true for dear old Ireland."

"Van Pelt, set all the sail she will carry!"

Zach and Dylan were quickly up into the rigging, back in

their natural element. Their laughter was sweet to hear. The line flew off the reel as the log was tossed. It revealed *Banshee* was flying along at thirteen knots. The wind was favorable for our voyage to Belfast. The hands who remembered the boys from before were amazed to see them so grown up. Zach had been the cook's mate, and Dylan the cabin boy. The hands all made a fuss over my sons. They loved the ship and all the attention.

We arrived in Belfast May 31, 1754. Our passage had taken only fifteen days. We would have two weeks to visit before our scheduled return trip. *Pride of Belfast*, the sister ship to *Pride of Charleston*, would be our consort.

It was good to see Father. He had aged shockingly in the past five years, in no small part to the death of my mother. He doted on Thomas and baby James. We had a good visit with Priscella's family. They were thrilled to meet their grandsons. Dylan and Zachary had gone to visit their parents on their farms.

Our round of visits was all too soon ended. We said our good-byes and set sail on June 15. Both Zachary's and Dylan's parents walked them to the dock. Their parting seemed much less painful than before; their hearts and homes were now in the Carolina wilderness. Father waited on the dock to watch us sail. I feared it would be the last time I would see him. I gave him a warm embrace and thanked him for everything. It left him red-faced and flustered. He managed to stammer, "I am proud of ye, my seventh son."

Clancy's booming voice pierced the morning air. "Good morning to ye, Thomas! The cargo and the lads are all aboard. They are in a fine fettle. We all feel as rich as lairds because of the company's bonus!"

Turning to the crew, I bellowed at them. "Aye, ye scurvy

wharf rats, I hope you have not already spent it in debauchery!"

The cargo was all aboard and stowed. *Pride of Belfast* was moored behind us, well laden and ready to sail.

"That slab-sided slug of a floating lumber yard will slow down the lovely *Banshee*."

"Aye, that is true, Clancy. But she carries a mountain of trade goods. It is as father has wished it. We will take the northern passage to Halifax, then down the American coast."

"There may be ice islands about in those waters soon."

"Aye, but it is much closer and faster for us to reach the plantation. We need to tend the crops so poor sailor men like you can receive a fat dividend."

"Now you are speaking to me heart, Thomas."

"McNamara, muster the crew on deck for sailing. Dylan, with respects to the master of *Belfast*, we are ready to sail. He is to watch for my signal."

"Aye, aye, sir!"

"Thomas, all passengers aboard, your honor."

"Mr. Clancy, you have my blessing to sail when you are ready."

"Aye, sir. Mr. Moore, cast off, if you please. Zachary, hoist *Belfast's* signal to prepare to sail. Van Pelt, you great lumbering Dutchman, set the jib to bring her head around."

Once *Banshee's* head was around, we were ready to depart.

"Van Pelt, topsails, if you please. Zachary, is that floating lumber yard coming around?"

"Aye, sir. They are swinging before the wind and setting sail."

"Patrick McNamara, do you think you could find it in your

heart to find our way out of the Lough of Belfast?"

"Aye, sir, with my eyes shut, in a heavy fog, with a broken rudder."

"Set the fore and aft main sails, Van Pelt."

Soon we reached the mouth of Lough Belfast. Rather than sailing south down the Irish Sea, we steered for the North Channel. By mid-morning we had the Giant's Causeway in sight to port. Priscella had never seen it. I showed it to Thomas and James, but they didn't seem too impressed. Noon saw Malin Head to port. It would be our last sight of Ireland.

We would use the westerly breezes to make a steady southwestern course for Halifax. It was sweet sailing across the North Atlantic. It was kind this time of year, but could be the devil in the winter. We met a home-ward bound packet which came within hailing distance. They warned us of ice islands twenty leagues ahead. We doubled the masthead lookouts and took a reef in the topsails. At dusk that night the mainmast lookout caught a glimpse of sail or ice to the west-northwest. The foremast lookout confirmed it.

We could not heave to for the night, as the sea bottom was far too deep to anchor. We would proceed with the jib and a double-reefed main topsail for the night. *Belfast* was to follow in our wake. Lookouts were rotated every two hours in the mastheads, and a hand in the bow.

After midnight, a heavy fog settled over us. We fired a leeward swivel gun so *Belfast* would know where we were. They answered promptly with another gun. If ice was seen ahead, we were to fire one rocket. If it was to windward, we were to fire two rockets, three for leeward. The fog intensified before dawn. Tension on *Banshee* was high. We could sense ice, but could not see it. Clancy stood nervously in the bow next to the lookout.

"Ice dead ahead! Ice dead ahead!"

"Port the helm hard over. Fire one rocket!"

A huge ice island loomed ahead, fine on our starboard bow, as *Banshee* turned sharply to port. We passed within forty feet of the iceberg, but we knew the submerged base extended out from the sides.

Clancy ran to the stern with a speaking trumpet, bellowing to *Belfast* to port her helm. A distinct "Aye, aye!" came through the fog. *Belfast* came on steadily. The much larger, heavily laden ship was not so nimble in answering her helm. Her turn to port was agonizingly slow.

We heard a grinding crash as the starboard bow of *Belfast* splintered into the towering mountain of ice. Her great masts whipped forward, ripping out their rigging, then sagging back, before falling overboard to port. The great ship split open at her bow, with the cold sea rushing in to the shattered hull. Cries to abandon ship were heard through the fog. Gratings, barrels and debris were thrown overboard. There had been no time to lower a boat. The hull of *Belfast* came to rest on the shoulder of the ice, and the flood of icy water rushed aft through the doomed ship. Within minutes, she was down by the stern and slipped stern-first into the sea.

We ordered two boats away to search for survivors. Of the thirty men of her crew, we found only five left alive. The likelihood of other ice in the area made it mandatory that we move along carefully and not linger in the ice field. We sailed on in gloomy silence.

John Cook fed the five half-drowned men, and gave them hot water strengthened with rum. They were given dry clothes, hammocks and heavy wool blankets. Their shaking was as much from shock as the cold. They were not able to speak more than to mumble single word answers. It would be days before they could talk about that night. It affected all of us in profound ways.

As daylight brought an end to the horrors of the night, we carefully added more sail to try to clear the last of the deadly ice field. By late afternoon, it appeared the worst was behind us. However, when darkness returned, we resumed our previous caution. The next day showed we were clear of the ice islands. We increased our daytime speed to all *Banshee* would carry, but again used great caution at night. We were all still in shock at the loss of the great ship and her crew.

By July 2, the approaches to Halifax harbor were in sight. The harbor pilot came on board and guided us into the great anchorage. A whole fleet could shelter there. We sent word by the packet brig back to Belfast with the grave news. The five survivors chose to continue with us and return to Belfast when her voyage was complete.

Our trip from Halifax to Georgetown was somber. Edward debarked there with those of us bound for the plantation. We bid farewell to our friends and relatives aboard *Banshee*. As our scow shouldered its way up the Pee Dee our mood lightened. It was good to be coming back to our home in the wilderness.

Mark met us at Cheraw Landing with the best wagons and draft horses. We arrived home just before dark. Charlotte had prepared a wonderful meal of ham, green beans, sweet potatoes and corn bread. All the hands were there. Ashley was large with child, due in only a month. We told of our visit to Ireland and the news from home. They gave us the news of the summer there on the plantation, which for the most part was uneventful. Before everyone left, I told them of the loss of the *Pride of Belfast*. They sat in stunned silence as they digested the news. Our many joys were now touched with the brush of sorrow at the loss of Artie, the *Belfast*, and the horrors of the ice island.

I surveyed each plantation and found things in good order. We now coordinated our efforts to clear two more acres for indigo at Gray Wolf. With all of us working together and all eight oxen pulling, the job was quickly done. The logs were piled along the creek. The ground was plowed and harrowed. We cleared the pine from five acres joining our pasture, leaving the hardwoods. The native grasses would soon fill the gaps. We added the pine logs to the pile along the creek. We cleared, plowed and harrowed two more acres each at Harrington and Quick farms.

One afternoon, there seemed to be some activity around the Harrington house. Mark came striding out of the house as proud as a peacock.

"I'm a father! It is a healthy girl. Ashley is fine."

"What is her name, Mark?"

"Oh, we have named her Rebecca, for my mother. She has brown hair and eyes."

We had to fend for ourselves for supper, as the women were still occupied with the birth. We were excited for Mark.

Fall harvest proceeded well. The corn bins were full of grain and the lofts full of stalks. Our barrels were filled with more than enough cornmeal for our needs, and they ground sixteen barrels for the neighbors. Keenan had built and sold the barrels. The tobacco crop was soon hanging in the curing barns over the slowly smoking fires. The quality looked even better than usual.

The twenty-eight acres of indigo were harvested and processed. It was a nauseating job, only brightened by the value of the finished product. We filled fourteen barrels of indigo. The Irish and sweet potatoes were dug and stored in the cellars.

The weather was good so we sowed twenty-four acres of wheat and oats. A few days after planting, we had a good, slow, soaking two inch rain. It would be enough to get the grain off to a good start.

We packed forty-two barrels of prime tobacco. We loaded it and the indigo into our wagons and hitched up the oxen. We spent the night at Cheraw Landing. The next day our armed scow arrived with an armed crew. Tom Red Hat and twelve of his men accompanied us. We headed down river at dawn. A strange craft appeared under Gardner's Bluff, but quickly rowed up into Crooked Creek. We had no other problems. The prices for indigo and tobacco were off a little due to a large harvest, but we still received $7,000. A full profit share was $85.

12

JANUARY OF 1755 MARKED the beginning of our sixth year in the Carolina wilderness. We had carved out a home and a degree of prosperity and security. For the first time, we felt that security threatened.

Reports were coming down from the northern colonies that the French had begun arming several of the Indian tribes and incited them to make war on the English settlers. So far, there had not been any large scale attacks reported. The attacks were far away from our homes. The Cheraw tribe was composed of peaceful landowners and farmers who lived much as we did. They farmed enough to meet their needs and had always been good neighbors. There were some Cherokee who lived in our area, but only a few. But to the northwest, there were huge Cherokee settlements. Like the Cheraw, they were mostly peaceable. They lived in cabins, raised crops and livestock. Things seemed quiet for now.

Keenan was busy making barrels, ox yokes, buckets and other useful things. He made respectable furniture, and knew which woods to select for their beauty and function. Sean repaired all the metal objects that needed fixing, and made the hoops for Keenan's barrels. He also made iron rims for wheels. He kept all of our firearms in top shape, and melted enough lead to keep us well supplied with bullets.

Dylan, Zachary, Logan, Jimmy, Jack and Nathan worked clearing more land. We could not manage any more indigo than we had now, but there was room for more tobacco, corn and grain. They cleared five acres on the Harrington farm and plowed and harrowed it for planting in the spring. They piled the logs along the creek. Five acres were added at both the Quick farm and Gray Wolf.

Edward said reports were coming down from the north about raids by Huron and Ottawa along the northwestern frontier. Relations between England and France had rapidly deteriorated. Father had sent word to watch for increased commerce raiding by French privateers. The troubles were becoming somewhat more real, but were still far away. We proceeded with our spring chores just as we always had done.

In July, during one of our sunset talks on the front porch, Priscella revealed to me that she was expecting another child sometime in early March. I was thrilled and quite pleased with myself.

That summer, we had an even dozen Cheraw Indians working for us. It was a tremendous help. Keenan and Mark both bought gaited horses to assist them with their overseer responsibilities in comfort. I had noticed that Keenan was riding over to Grant's plantation rather often. Logan confided that Keenan was seeing Constance Grant. He was nineteen and she was eighteen. I had no objection, but I wasn't so sure about Mr. Grant. Keenan finally asked me for my blessing to ask her to marry him. Of course, I agreed. To my amazement, Mr. Grant agreed. A wedding date was set for November, after harvest and before hog killing time. This was the Carolinas! We had to be practical, after all. Keenan asked Sean to stand up with him. Constance asked Ashley Cunningham.

To my surprise, Sean came by within a week to ask my blessing to marry Sarah Red Hat, Thomas's oldest daughter. Sean was twenty-one and she was sixteen. I decided I had better go with him to talk to Red Hat. He did not object, but instead asked a bride price of three new axes, a gaited horse and $20. In return, Red Hat would deed to the newlyweds sixty acres of his land that joined the north border of the Quick farm. Sean accepted. He made the axes himself, and bought a fine gaited horse from Mr. Grant for the princely sum of $100! They would share the wedding date with Keenan and Constance.

The Methodist minister arrived the last Friday nigh of November. The Saturday morning double ceremony was the first wedding held in the new church. All the neighbors and Red Hat's village were there. There was a huge feast with a hog cooked in the ground and all the trimmings. Keenan honeymooned in the Quick farm house, while Sean and Sarah stayed in a special lodge in Red Hat's village.

We continued to hear stories of Indian raids and French privateers in other places, but they were all far away and did not directly affect us. That would soon change.

The year 1756 began eventfully. Logan Perkins was twenty.

He had met Mary Red Hat during Sean's courtship of her sister, Sarah. She was a beautiful young woman of sixteen, and Logan had fallen deeply in love. He met with me asking my opinion and blessing for him to approach Tom Red Hat about marrying his daughter. I agreed, and offered to go with him to meet with Red Hat. The chief liked the idea. He asked a bride price of a pair of female oxen, and $20. In turn, he would deed to Logan and Mary sixty acres joining Sean and Sarah.

Later that same week, Jack Harrington and Esther Quick came to see me. They also wanted to get married. What was in our well water? It seemed to be contagious. They asked if they could buy forty acres of undeveloped land adjoining the Perkins brothers. They both still wanted to work for me, but to start something for themselves on the side. They had saved enough money to buy a yoke of oxen, some basic farm implements, tools, and household goods. I was pleased, and of course, offered my blessing.

The Methodist minister agreed to come the first Friday in February for a Saturday wedding.

"Brother Turner, I fear there are those among your neighbors who would object if Jack and Esther, being Negroes, are married in the church building. What do you think if I do a second ceremony at your farm afterwards?"

"Aye, Brother Browning. You are in the right of it. In my own mind, God loves all of His children. But there are those near us who would strongly disagree. Let's do it just like you said."

I rode with Jack and Logan to Cheraw. There was no problem with Logan getting a license and posting the banns. It was a bit more complicated for Jack. He had to show his emancipation papers, and those of Esther. I had to sign an affidavit that they were the same persons named in the emancipation papers. The judge reviewed the documents and said that as they were both free blacks, they would be allowed to marry. I helped him purchase a license and post the banns. I stopped by the attorney's office and had him draw up a deed for the forty acres of the former Quick farm directly across from the Perkins brothers and registered the sale in the clerk's office. It was rare enough for there to be free Negroes, but for them to own land was extremely rare.

Reverend Browning arrived as expected, and held a nice wedding for Logan and Mary Saturday morning. After a noontime banquet, some of us reassembled at Gray Wolf house where he married Jack and Esther. They both followed folk custom and jumped over a broom handle at the end of the service. We held a special feast for them that all our plantation families attended, as well as Red Hat's village. The licenses were signed, returned to the District Clerk's office and duly recorded. Any children born to Jack and Esther would be free-born.

On a frosty morning, March 7, 1756, Priscella delivered our first daughter. She was a beautiful little girl with a strong pair of lungs. She had auburn fuzz and dark blue eyes. We named her Jane. From the first moment I saw her, she captured my love. As I took her from Charlotte to hold, she grabbed my finger and my heart. She was precious. I felt so protective of her. I felt the same way about the boys, but there was just something more intense about my feelings for baby Jane. I think it was how much of Priscella I saw in her, and my love for Priscella spilled over on Jane. What ever it was, she had me by the finger her whole life. Her brothers were somewhat disinterested in the new arrival. I spent more time with them, and took them with me most places I went. They were growing up to be "Dada's boys," and I must admit I loved that.

We all worked together to get the spring crops planted. We pitched in and helped Sean, Logan, and Jack plant their small fields. It was obvious they were proud to be land owners. I was proud to see our community growing and flourishing. We hired even more help from our Cheraw Indian neighbors to cultivate and harvest the crops than ever before. We needed the help, and they found many uses for the extra money. Some of them had gone beyond just planting small crops for their own needs, but small acreages of cash crops, too.

In mid-summer we got word from Georgetown that France and Britain were formally at war. The French and Indians had spilled much blood in the Ohio valley. The British had suffered terrible losses all along the northwestern frontier. Indians were raiding deep into the Alleghenies, striking isolated farms and small villages. The British seemed powerless to stop them.

After hearing the news, I invited all the neighbor men to the church building for a meeting. We were so far from any British garrison, and so isolated by geography, that should the Cherokees or Creeks raid our area we would be virtually defenseless. I proposed that we organize a Marlboro County militia. We sent out the word that we would meet in one week there at the Turner's Crossing church at noon on Saturday.

The meeting's attendance far exceeded my expectations. Homes and farms from a fifty mile radius were represented there. In all, seventy men were present.

Many had come the night before and had camped on the plantation, while others rode in that morning. At noon we served huge kettles of stew and countless pans of cornbread in the school yard. After eating, we assembled in the church.

Discussion continued much of the afternoon. It was

decided to divide the county into four districts. There seemed to be natural dividing lines. The North District was designated Company A of the Marlboro County Regiment. Each plantation would appoint or elect a sergeant and a corporal. Each company would elect a captain and lieutenants. The A Company elected Allen Altman as captain. There would be approximately fifty men available for service in his company.

The South District would be Company B. They chose Jonathan Moore as their captain. They could muster seventy-two men. The East District was Company C, or Bright's Company. They were centered at Brightsville, and William Bright was their captain. They could count on about eighty men.

The West District, or Turner's District, was Company D. It was often called Turner's Company or Gray Wolf Company. In time, we would be known as the Devil Wolves. I was elected to serve as captain, but when all four companies' officers convened, I was elected as regimental major. Tom Red Hat was made captain. Our company could muster ninety men. This gave us a regimental strength of almost three hundred men fit for duty.

In the time of alarm, the company which was threatened would send riders to the other three companies if the threat was more than their company could contain. Each company would be responsible for scouting in their district. Each man would be responsible for his own weapons and would have thirty ready-made cartridges at hand, and whatever provisions he could quickly carry. Our company would dress in buckskins, and don our wolf skin or similar hats. They were each to keep a filled canteen and a pouch with jerky and parched corn hanging by their rifle and cartridges, plus a wool blanket. Any personal belongings could be rolled inside the blanket to minimize noise.

Our garments would help us disappear into the forests.

Turner Shipping and Trade sent four four-pounder howitzers. The howitzers were lighter than cannons, but had a limited range. They were fitted with a special carriage that could easily be drawn by a single horse. The carriages were much narrower than regular cannon carriages, and could be maneuvered through forest trails. They also came with a set of "man ropes" that could be fitted over the shoulders of half a dozen men if horses were unavailable or the terrain was too rough to use them. They also supplied us with two kegs of special powder, solid four pound shot and canister. Our office in Georgetown would send immediate word of any danger from the coast or on the Pee Dee. Now armed and organized loosely, we felt we were no longer alone in the wilderness.

As fall of 1756 approached, the war continued. French warships and privateers regularly raided merchant ships. Indian depredations continued to the north. The last of the British forts on the northwestern frontier fell to the French and their Indian allies. But at Turner's Crossing, there was a sense of security.

Mark proudly announced that he would be a father again around the first of March. Logan, Sean, Keenan and Jack had lost no time in starting their families either. The community of our plantation was growing by leaps and bounds.

Harvest was bountiful. Our barns were full. Priscella's carefully tended apple trees were coming into full production and providing us with fresh apples and cider, and dried apples for the winter.

We shipped our largest crops yet of indigo and tobacco to Georgetown. The price was stronger than usual due to disrupted supplies because of the war. Our crop sold for just over $20,000. I was thrilled and surprised! The bonus was $225 each. The hands had by now accumulated substantial savings.

The news in Georgetown was not good. The fall of the last British forts had opened a highway to invasion from Canada all the way to the Alleghenies, leaving a trail of bloody ground and burned farms behind.

As I had been elected regimental major, I appointed Mark as Lieutenant to serve as my adjutant and Sean as Lieutenant of Artillery. Mark and I made an inspection tour to each of the other three companies to evaluate their readiness. We found them overall to be well prepared and willing to fight if necessary.

We had survived 1756 unscathed by war, but better prepared if it should come. Before long, we knew it had come to our doorsteps.

As January 1757 dawned, I was determined to drill our militia company. I knew they could all handle their guns, but wanted them to practice volley firing and teach them how to use the howitzer. I sent word around for as many of the company who were able to attend. Men came from Red Hat's village, and from the Grant, Irby, Smith, and Douglas plantations. The ferryman from Cheraw Landing, Ian Llewellyn, and his three sons came, too. You could count on a Welshman to be plenty scrappy!

We had the men form in three lines, with the front rank kneeling. As the front rank fired, they dropped behind the third to begin reloading. The next rank knelt and fired on command, and moved to the rear, and the last line, which was now the first, repeated the process. By this time the first to fire were reloaded. Next we practiced it the opposite direction where the first line to fire held their place, as the rear rank moved to the front and knelt to fire, and so on, so the line was slowly advancing. They quickly grasped this concept.

We showed them how to deploy in a skirmish line. In this, they were scattered several feet apart laying down to fire, with a second row behind them, shooting between the gaps in the front row. We also taught them how to conduct an orderly fighting retreat. I knew that the men would not stand much of a chance against French regulars led by well-trained officers in a bayonet charge, or against charging cavalry. But if we ever met such a force, we would need to know how to get ourselves out of a mess.

We next taught those who did not know how to fire the howitzers, for if our gun crews fell, others would have to take their place. This is where Sean was invaluable.

"All of ye listen now. First you make sure you have your tools. This is a rammer and this is a sponge. These guns are light enough you will not need crowbars to move them for aiming. Make sure you have cartridges ready-made or dry powder near to hand, but not too close to the gun. These linen bags are made to hold a pound of powder. Ram it home all the way to the bottom of the barrel. Place a four pound round shot or a canister of shot on top of the powder. If you don't ram it home firmly on top of the powder, it may well kill you and your whole gun crew. Keep a length of slow match close to hand or in a bucket, but keep it away from the powder! Clear the vent on your gun with this awl. Push it home until you feel it pierce the linen bag. There will be powder on the end of it if you got it right. The awl is copper. If you use iron or steel, it could spark and kill ye. And that would prove a mess for the rest of us to clean up! Next, fill the vent with fine powder from this horn. Make sure you have it lined up straight and the elevation adjusted with this quoin. The gun will thunder backwards when it is fired, so make sure your mates stand clear. The man who is to fire the gun should take the slow match in hand, and stick the end over the vent while standing to the side. Do ye have any questions?"

We had the Gray Wolf hands take the first turn to show them how to do it. They picked out a large dead tree about 400 yards away, and readied the gun. On Sean's signal, they fired, just barely missing the tree. The second shot flew straight and stuck the trunk with a loud "thonk." We moved them to 100 yards and had them demonstrate what a load of canister could do. Each group took their turn, doing rather well, including Red Hat's men. Just as one of the last groups to take their turn prepared to fire, one of the Irby's men chased his hat in front of the loaded howitzer. Sean grabbed the gun captain's hand just before he set the match to the vent.

"Look out!"

We could all feel the tension as we realized what had almost happened, but Sean saved the day with his humor.

"Just like an Englishman to try to get to heaven before the Irish!"

The crowd laughed and relaxed, as the man discreetly retrieved his hat. We broke up the meeting with some cold cider and shortbread.

Edward brought me up-to-date on what little news there was to tell. We discussed that perhaps we could diversify the plantation a little more by adding a tannery. Tanned leather was hard to find and expensive. The few cattle we slaughtered could not provide enough work to keep a tanner busy, but it might work if we bought the neighbors cowhides. As tanneries tend to smell awful and need lots of water, I suggested we could locate it at Turner's Landing, and the tanner could live in the small cabin already there.

We also talked about the increasing trade and traffic along the road through Turner's Crossing and the possible need for an inn and tavern there. We could build it ourselves and run it with some extra help. We agreed to proceed with both projects as time permitted around the farm work.

Finally, I broached the idea of buying an additional one thousand acres of forest land that joined ours on the south from the Irby's holdings. They had never done anything with it, and did not intend to develop it. They had offered it at a good price of one and a half silver dollars per acre.

When we returned home, I met with the Irbys and traveled with them to Cheraw to transfer the land and register the deed. With the added acres, our plantation was now over two thousand acres, but still mostly forest.

Once the crops were adequately started, we began work on the inn. It was situated next to the church on a nice large tract of land. We cleared the timber off the lot. A few pretty hardwoods were saved to shade the building. There weren't enough logs there for the whole inn, as it was fairly large. We harvested the pines off five acres next to our existing pasture to supply the rest. As usual for pasture, we left all the hardwoods and the pine stumps. We used all squared and mitered logs under Keenan's direction. There was a large central room with a fireplace on one end, with the kitchen on the other end, and quarters for the inn keeper. There was a second story where all the guest rooms were located, four on each side of the hall. Each upstairs room had a small glass window that opened and closed, with working shutters. Keenan found some excellent yellow poplar he used to make tables, benches and chairs for the main room. There was a deep porch running the front of the inn facing the road. We also built a barn and pens that would accommodate travelers' horses, with hay and feed storage.

We found a family to run the inn. The father was Adam Calhoun, his wife Elizabeth, and their children Matilda, Stephen, and Bonnie. Elizabeth would be in charge of the kitchen and laundry, with her daughters helping her. Stephen, who was fourteen, would run the livery.

After consultation with my brothers and Father, it was decided to open our own bank at Turner's Crossing. We had small banks in Kingston, Charleston and Georgetown, so this one would fit nicely. We built a sturdy stone one-story building next to the store. It had glass windows and working shutters that opened and closed from inside. The outside was protected with iron bars that Sean made. The door was heavy oak hung on hinges built into the rock walls, and reinforced with heavy decorative iron straps. Inside was a teller's desk, an office, and a back room built of stone with a stone roof above it, which housed a London-made safe. The roof of the bank was of slate that we bought. My brother William's son, Isham, had worked at the bank in Kingston. He would come to run the bank here. It was called simply the Bank of Turner's Crossing.

By the end of 1757, Turner's Crossing had a population of thirty free white men and women, several children, and a handful of free blacks. Although surrounded by miles of forested wilderness, we were carving out a comfortable, safe, permanent home.

13

OUR FEARS OF AN ATTACK by either French or Indians did not materialize, although parts of the colonies had suffered grievously. We enjoyed peace, and so far, it had not proven to be an illusion. In the early months of 1758, Logan and Mary had a daughter, Abigail. Jack and Esther had a little boy they named "Freedom."

Priscella went into labor on a cold March night. We sent for Betty and Charlotte. When they arrived, Charlotte seemed worried when she checked Priscella. The baby was coming breech, bottom first! She said she had delivered a breech once before, but predicted it would be a very difficult labor. Priscella struggled and pushed with all her might, as Betty helped push down from Priscella's abdomen. The pain was horrible, but she bore it stoically. She knew if she didn't push the baby out, both the baby and she might die. Finally, the boy baby emerged none the worse for the wear. Priscella was weak to the point of exhaustion, but they held the baby up for her to nurse. We named the baby John, and he, too, became a special part of our lives, as had the other children.

Our plantation and community continued to prosper. The mill was enlarged to handle larger amounts of corn and wheat, as grain was being brought in from miles around. The school was well attended and usually full. The inn proved to be a surprising success, and always had at least a few guests, and was often near capacity. The smith and carpentry shop stayed busy, and brought in business from the whole area. The work for the plantation got first priority, as was our agreement. Keenan was able to tend to his responsibilities as overseer of the Quick farm by putting in very full days. There was always stock stabled at the livery. The store was crammed full of merchandise, which was regularly replenished. The bank also proved a success. We were apparently not the only ones who had grown tired of the trip to Cheraw to do our banking. We had applied for and been approved for a Cheraw District Clerk's branch with a man to handle legal documents, licenses and fees. He was given a desk in the bank.

We continued to clear more land for corn, wheat and oats each year. The acres planted to sweet potatoes and Irish potatoes doubled. We added six acres of tobacco and two of indigo each year. We tried to clear the pines from ten acres for pasture each year, too. The timber was a major source of our income, and we had barely scratched the surface on the vast forests around us. We added a few more oxen and milk cows, and draft horses, too. Our freighting business was always busy. The tannery slowly grew busier. Mr. Jones, the tanner, made trips every three months to pick up dried, salted hides from the neighbors. He did some harness building and repair, as well as general leather work of a rough sort. He was not a shoemaker.

When the company scow arrived in the fall of 1758, it brought welcome news. The British and colonial militias had recovered the forts along the frontier one by one. The British had captured the massive French fortress of Louisburg, which had been their most formidable stronghold on the American continent. They had also captured Fort Duquesne, which they renamed Fort Pitt. The crowning victory had come when General Wolfe had led an expedition against the seemingly impregnable fortress of Quebec and defeated the French. The British navy had gained the upper hand over the French navy and their privateers.

Zachary Hawkins married Carolina Bright, daughter of William Bright in 1759. It was a big step for the son of a tenant farmer, and former cook's mate, to marry the daughter of one of the most successful men in Marlboro County. I sold him forty acres of forest land from the Harrington farm. They built a nice home there.

Dylan, who was twenty in 1759, was a fine young man. We depended heavily on him on the plantation. He married a strikingly beautiful young Cherokee woman. They bought forty acres joining Zachary and Carolina. I would have guessed that they would own adjoining farms, for they were still as close as brothers.

Late in 1760, I was blessed with another son, Moses. He arrived without the drama of his brother, John. He was a fine little boy who resembled my father.

We received word that summer Father had passed away. He had bequeathed to me the company's 35 percent ownership of the plantation and all the enterprises associated with it. I would still hold my shares in Turner Shipping and Trade.

The 1760 census showed there were forty-three adult white men and women in Turner's Crossing, plus children, and sixteen free black men and women, plus their children. Our community had become a small town.

In 1762, the Lord blessed Priscella and me with another son, Mark. He was red headed and blue-eyed like his siblings. Mark and Ashley had the misfortune of a stillborn infant. They handled their loss stoically. He was buried in the cemetery on the Harrington farm.

We built a well-made stone bridge over Phill's Creek that was two lanes wide. Its wide arching supports were strong and should hold up well against the occasional flood waters. Mr. Bright built a timber bridge over Antioch Creek, so that it was possible to travel from Cheraw Landing to Brightsville without getting wet. We provided weekly freight service between Cheraw and Brightsville, with connections to Georgetown by company scow. We shipped large amounts of timber from Turner's Landing. We had begun to develop the land I had bought from the Irby's estate on Beaver Creek.

In 1763, we received joyous news that the British and French had signed the Treaty of Paris, ending the war. Britain received all of Canada, except a few small islands France retained for fishing rights. Spain, who had been unfortunate enough to ally itself to France, traded their claim to Florida for land west of the Mississippi. The Creeks, and those bands of Cherokee who had joined them, made peace also. We celebrated a great feast in honor of the end of the hostilities. King George III had ascended to the throne, and had not yet descended into madness. Would peace and prosperity last? Only time would tell. But our Garden of Eden would not escape the next time.

The harbingers of future conflict first began to surface in 1763. With peace within the empire, George III determined to increase revenues by squeezing the colonies. With the French threat temporarily resolved, and peace at hand, the colonies were not receptive to new taxes. The American colonies were most vocal of their resentment.

The Proclamation of 1763 prohibited colonists from settling west of the Alleghenies, in order to keep from antagonizing the Indians. But the thrust of American colonization was, and always would be, relentlessly westward. And besides, there were already many colonists west of the Alleghenies. What of them?

When George Glenville became prime minister in 1764, it became evident that the government primarily viewed the colonies as a source of revenue. They existed to provide raw materials and sales outlets for the great mercantile empire, not necessarily to prosper for themselves.

The first in a string of increasingly disagreeable laws was the Sugar Act. It enforced a tariff on sugar from the Caribbean sugar plantations to the colonies, or between the colonies themselves. Sugar grown on the lower Pee Dee could not be sold in Virginia or Massachusetts without a high tariff. This was to keep the price of sugar flowing into England cheap at the expense of others.

The next was the Stamp Act of 1765. It required the placement of revenue stamps on all legal documents, and many luxury items. A deed, a will, a marriage license or land survey was not valid unless carrying a revenue stamp. This tax was not applied except in the colonies. British citizens in England did not have to pay this tax, but their kinsmen in the American colonies did.

The colonies had no legislative voice to speak before Parliament. Thus came the cry of "No taxation without representation!" It stirred the imaginations of many loyal subjects in the colonies.

The South Carolina Assembly had long been organized and met in Charleston to advise the Royal Governor, and to provide a voice from the colony to the crown. The assembly had been granted some latitude to settle local disputes that did not involve Parliament's rights or the prerogatives of the King. On the subject of the Stamp Act, the Assembly clearly expressed its displeasure to the Governor. To his credit, the Governor did not much like it himself. He would relay the Assemblies' displeasure to Lord Glenville's cabinet.

Our colonial neighbors to the north in Virginia were aroused enough to call a meeting of colonial delegates to what would be called "The Stamp Act Congress." Nine colonies sent delegates there. They condemned the Stamp Act, but then went further to claim that Parliament had no right to tax the colonies at all! The Stamp Act was repealed in the Declaratory Act of 1766, but Parliament simultaneously reasserted its authority to tax the colonies without their consent.

Since the Stamp Act was repealed, Glenville's government levied new taxes on many things, including tea, glass, paint, paper and lead. This led to a wide boycott of these things within the colonies. At Turner's Crossing, we found many ways around the tax and avoided buying taxed items. Colonists suddenly found more interest in drinking coffee, or doing without tea. There was a fairly brisk business in smuggling untaxed tea. Lead could be recycled. Glass was not a necessity. Parchment could be made of vellum, and many buildings went unpainted. The English merchants quickly noted a huge decline in sales, which was promptly brought to Glenville's attention. This caused the repeal of the import duties in 1770.

Our hot-headed Yankee neighbors in Boston vented their frustration on British soldiers with snow balls and cat-calls. The frustrated and out-numbered soldiers ordered the hecklers to disperse. They were answered with a shower of insults, snowballs and stones. They fired their muskets into the angry mob, killing five, and dispersing the rest with their bayonets.

These developments did not go unnoticed at Turner's Crossing, or anywhere else in the colonies. I was gravely worried. The local sentiment, as well as across South Carolina and the colonies as a whole, was quickly souring on our British overlords. Most of us knew how the government dealt with unrest in Ireland and Scotland. We knew the consequences of being out of favor with the British. Many of us were Presbyterians, Methodist, Catholics, Irishmen, Scots or Welshmen. We knew the violence that could follow. It was bad enough to be second-class citizens. It was deadly to be vocal about it. My stomach churned as I feared our paradise of isolated freedom in the wilderness could be lost by events beyond my control.

I did not sleep well, and walked the floor deep in thought. We shared the house now only with our brood of children, which now included Mary born in 1766. Thomas was nineteen; James was seventeen; Jane was a precocious fourteen; John was only ten; Moses was eight; Mark was six, and there was baby Mary. Priscella sensed my restlessness and joined me.

"What troubles ye, husband?"

"It is many things, my dear. There is unrest in the land."

"Aye. I have felt it, too. Perhaps all will be well. We have been mostly untroubled so far."

"I hope so, my love. I feel that our life here is threatened by this unrest. We are so blest here with our family, our holdings, our friends, and our freedom that we did not have in Ireland. I just don't want to lose any of that."

The 1770 census showed Turner's Crossing had seventy-one adult white inhabitants, plus children, and twenty free black adults, plus their children. Our Marlboro County Volunteer Regiment had grown to four hundred men at arms. All four hundred were trained in Indian tactics, and British tactics. They could ambush and skirmish from the woods, or fight in line of battle if necessary. Our company was proficient in the use of our light artillery, and the whole regiment was trained and ready to fight. But who would we be fighting? Not the French. Perhaps the Indians. Perhaps British Regulars. The latter was almost unthinkable to raise arms against the King's troops.

Our community was well-established and prosperous. Our cultivated acres continued to increase, as did our acres for pasture. We rotated crops every year on all the crops except indigo, to prevent disease. We used manure and composted bedding straw for fertilizers. Between the three farms, and not counting the smaller plantings of Sean and the others, we had sizable acreage planted. We had sixty-four acres in indigo, over one hundred in tobacco, sixteen in potatoes, and over two hundred in wheat and oats. We had one hundred and eighty acres of improved pasture, and larger flocks of sheep, more hogs, more oxen, milk cows and draft horses. There was a brisk local market for our produce. We continued to send many dollars' worth of logs down to Georgetown, and our freight business, inn, store, mill, smith and carpenter shop were doing very well. The bank was growing, and even our tannery was doing well. All was well, and yet it was not.

There was a growing discomfort under the yoke of England. Some desired to be free of the English. Others desired only equal rights and representation with other English men. A few resented all change and wanted things to stay the way they were. They were the ones who had strong family ties to England, and they feared their loss of rank, privilege, wealth and influence with any change of the status quo.

Most of us were content to be subjects of King George, as long as his ministers did not interfere with us too much. The northern colonies were developing industries, especially textiles. Their goods were taxed if sent to England or other colonies, just to protect the monopoly of the English textile mills. The northerners agitated for radical change, while most in the south desired a more gradual transition to reform.

The writings of Thomas Paine circulated widely within the colonies, as did Benjamin Franklin's *Poor Richard's Almanac*. They had some influence on us. They at least caused us to question our allegiance to the crown. If we had the same status as English boroughs and counties, we would have a voice in the House of Commons. But we had no voice in our government. Slowly, almost imperceptibly, the public opinion was inching towards independence.

The Tea Act brought things to a boiling point. The venerable East India Company was able to sell tea in America directly to dealers of their choosing, duty-free. When American firms sold tea, it was heavily taxed. This especially angered those of us in the Turner Shipping and Trade Company, as we could not compete with the East India Company in British waters, and we were not allowed to conduct trade between British territory and foreign nations at all. We could not long survive the situation.

Our company, along with countless others, was forced to carry undeclared cargo to avoid the taxes. The more vulgar term for this was "smuggling." We kept a ship's manifest of taxed cargo, but concealed vast amounts of untaxed goods. This was common practice from Georgia to New England. Our indigo and tobacco could now be sold only in English ports, even if Belgium, France or Spain were paying much higher prices. The English merchants bought it, and without even repackaging it, sold it in foreign markets for huge profits that rightfully belonged to us.

We were allowed only to import English goods, even if better goods at cheaper prices could be obtained elsewhere. The greed of the government and the merchants was choking the colonies that were largely responsible for their wealth.

The New England traders, as well as all traders all along the American coast, could feel the noose tightening. The colonial merchants and planters felt cheated. Even the housewives felt resentment every time they had to pay inflated prices. Something must give soon.

In December 1773, the "Sons of Liberty" in Boston dressed as Indians and boarded East Indian ships in the harbor and cast their cargos of tea into the harbor. In response to this act of defiance, and others, Parliament passed what became known as "The Intolerable Acts." Boston harbor was closed. Massachusetts was placed under martial law. Colonist were forced to house and feed British troops against their will. All of the land west of the Alleghenies was placed under the jurisdiction of Canada! If this happened in Boston, the rest of us would not be far behind! Our peace and freedom were now directly threatened

In the early months of 1775, I decided that we needed a break. I invited all the Gray Wolf Plantation men on a hunting trip. My sons would join us. Thomas was almost twenty-four, James was twenty-two, Aaron was almost seventeen, John was pushing fifteen, and Moses was almost thirteen. Mark was only ten, and we left him behind, much to his displeasure. There were sixteen of us, clad in our buckskins and wolf and other skin hats. We looked like a Creek war band. We pushed northwest toward the mountains in search of deer and turkey. There were plenty around Turner's Crossing, but plenty of chores to do, too. We brought our gear very much as we would on the march with our militia company. We would sleep in wool blankets rolled in canvas wagon sheets to keep out the moisture. We passed Red Hat's land and pushed on until we came to the foothills above the upper Pee Dee.

The next morning, Dylan and Zach both bagged a turkey. We fried them in bacon grease and rolled in corn meal. It was delicious. Sean, Logan, and their sons went out looking for walnuts and came back with a story of a huge hornets nest. They said it was the largest they had ever seen. I thought their Irish imaginations were getting ahead of them, but they convinced the rest of us to go with them to see it. High up in a very old tall hickory tree was a hornets nest the size of a half-bushel basket! It had a thick stem holding it to the tree. I offered a silver dollar as a prize to the first one who could shoot the stem off from 30 yards. We backed off and began shooting from youngest to oldest. The first shooter missed the nest, limb and tree. We gave him quite a bit of good-natured teasing. The next shooter pierced the middle of the massive nest. We could hear an audible hum coming from inside it. One of the boys managed to hit the limb holding the nest, shaking the hornets up a bit more. Moses took his time, drew careful aim, and shot the stem off the nest, sending it crashing to the ground. As soon as it hit, it burst open, exploding to life with a dark cloud of angry hornets. The hornets swarmed towards the lingering cloud of gun smoke. Realizing our mistake too late, we ran like our pants were on fire! We laughed as we ran, swatting hornets off our faces and hands. They stung us again and again as we ran yelping in pain and laughing at our predicament. They finally quit chasing us just short of our camp. We collapsed in exhaustion on the ground with swollen faces, laughing until we wheezed. It would be a story that would grow with each retelling, and yet leave us doubled over in laughter.

As our world stumbled closer to open war with Britain, life went on around us. Thomas, Jr. met Rebecca Marion. Her father, Francis Marion, was a hero of the recent French and Indian War. He had led a retaliatory raid against the Creeks and Cherokees that halted their raids in western North Carolina and western South Carolina. He was a successful planter on the Santee River, and a delegate to the State Assembly. Thomas and Rebecca were married at the Marion plantation in June. They made their home on one hundred and sixty acres of the land I had bought from the Irbys that I gave them as a wedding gift.

We had learned at Thomas' wedding that gunfire had already erupted in Massachusetts at Concord and Bunker Hill. British troops were pouring into the northern colonies.

Times were changing. Where had the time gone? When Priscella and I had arrived at our home in the wilderness, we were younger than most of our children. We had seen our dreams fulfilled beyond our wildest expectations. We were close to all of our children and enjoyed them a great deal. The boys had grown up working side by side with me on the plantation, and they knew every aspect of the work. The girls had learned at their mother's side. All of them had attended our school, and could read and write well, as well as do their sums. The older boys had advanced in math and what science they could learn. We had read the Bible together almost every night of their lives, and their heroes had been Moses, David, Ruth and Esther. They were kind to others, honest, fair and respectful of other people and other's property. They had grown into children of whom we could be proud. I guessed it wouldn't be long until we had grandchildren. Our friends who had started on this adventure with us were still nearby and as close to us as family. They had married and had families, and in their own rights, had prospered and found happiness.

This place had been our "promised land." We shared readily with others, but would fiercely defend ourselves against any threat to our homes and prosperity. But now greed, ambition, pride, and a disregard for the rights of others was threatening to take it away. If there was any means to preserve our way of life peacefully, we would have it. But if peaceful means failed, we were ready to take up arms.

I represented Marlboro County at the Cheraw District Assembly. We discussed our options, and elected three delegates to send to the State Assembly in Charleston. The representatives in Charleston eloquently stated our grievances and our desire for peace. We asked that if there was to be taxation that there must be representation in Parliament. We asked for the rights common to all Englishmen. The Assembly sent delegates to the Continental Congress in Philadelphia.

The Congress addressed the issues one by one. They were united in the demand that we be given the rights common to all Englishmen, and that we be given representation in Parliament for all matters concerning the colonies and taxation. King George, Lord Glenville and Parliament thought these requests ridiculous and insubordinate. They were uniformly rejected.

The news from the northern colonies was bad. The British were blockading harbors and landing even more troops. There was little sympathy for our cause in England.

When the Cheraw District Assembly met in May, 1776, we voted to declare our district independent of the Crown. We were one of the first Assemblies to do so, but many more would follow. On July 4, 1776, the Declaration of Independence was adopted by the Continental Congress in Philadelphia. It was now up to the individual colonies to ratify the Declaration. At least on paper, we were free from England. Now blood would be required to make it a reality.

War would come to our door sooner than we thought. On June 28, 1776, the British navy launched an attack on Charleston harbor. Their heavy warships had to pass under the great guns of Fort Moultrie. With incredible arrogance, the British sailed straight into the harbor's mouth. There were led by a heavy 36 gun frigate, which opened fire with its 12 pounders. The shot bounced off the well-made fort and did not frighten the defenders within the heavy stone walls. The fort's 42 pounders opened a devastating barrage. The frigate was so badly damaged it was unable to steer and drifted aimlessly onto a sand bar, striking her colors.

Close behind the frigate came three huge 74 gun ships armed with 18 and 24 pounders. Their guns raised clouds of dust and debris from Fort Moultrie. They intended to beat it into a pile of submissive rubble. Although damaging the fort, the 42 pounders opened with a violent response. They were now firing heated shot into the tinder dry floating fortresses, with their dry canvas and tarred rigging. Within minutes the great warships were broken and engulfed in flames. All three ended their days in the waters of Charleston harbor. The remainder of the squadron which had not yet entered the harbor retreated for the safety of the sea. Death was at our doorstep.

Colonel Francis Marion, Thomas' father-in-law, was commander of the militias from the Santee all the way to the North Carolina line. He called for all the militia commanders to assemble at Georgetown on October 1, 1776. I took Thomas with me in a company scow to the meeting where we stayed with my brother, Edward. We provided the offices of Turner Shipping and Trade as a meeting place. We learned that warships had made a demonstration up the Hudson River with the thunder and lightening of their guns, but had failed to impress the local citizens. General George Washington had command of the Continental army assembled in New York. Our army had suffered severe losses, but was still fighting. Elsewhere, the British had recruited Indian allies to join the Tories. The Tories were colonists loyal to the Crown. They raided down the frontier as far as North Carolina, burning towns and farms, and killing anyone who supported independence. The Huron, Ottawa and Creek allied with the British. The Choctaw and Cherokee were divided. The Cheraw of our district were resolutely united with us.

The volunteers along the Santee were to support Charleston. The militia on the lower Pee Dee was to support Georgetown if it were attacked. The regiment from Cheraw and Columbia were to guard the western frontier. Our regiment was to watch for the British advancing from the north and watch for raids by Indians coming down from North Carolina. All regiments were to observe and suppress with "the minimum effective force" the activity of the Loyalist.

We returned to find harvest in full swing. The corn cribs were full. We milled extra barrels of corn meal and hid it at remote places on the plantation where it would stay dry, along with barrels of flour, dried beans, and smoked and salted pork. We also hid extra powder, shot and muskets carefully sealed against moisture. If we were raided, we did not want all our stores taken.

Each of the four companies of the Marlboro County Volunteer Regiment established regular patrols in their districts. Mr. Jones, the tanner kept watch for any enemy movement up the river. He had a good horse that could carry him quickly up the creek to home. He was also to set a signal fire, as we had discussed. The smoke could be seen a long way in the day time, but should appear to be a normal farming activity to any casual observer. My sons Aaron and Moses, kept watch on Beaver Creek. This would give us another ten miles of warning. They both kept horses there, as well as a signal fire at the ready. Red Hat's men patrolled paths known only to them. Nothing moved in the forest without their knowledge.

Our indigo harvest and processing was completed. We had a huge crop. The tobacco was dried, smoked and barreled. We hauled it to Cheraw Landing and loaded it on two heavily armed scows. We stopped at Snow Island until a company ship from Georgetown would arrive to give us the all clear to proceed down the river. The next morning, another armed scow loaded with armed men arrived to escort us the last leg of the journey.

When we arrived, we found *Banshee* tied up at the company wharf. The crew was taking on stores.

"Look alive, Brian Clancy! Step lively, McNamara! Van Pelt, you old Dutchman! Ahoy, Charles Moore and Conner McLean! Avast there, John Cook!"

It was wonderful to see my old shipmates. They had brought us here twenty-seven years before! They looked more worried than happy to see me.

Clancy growled, "Thomas Turner! Proud to see your lordship! Now if you would move your lubberly backside, and let real sailormen load your cargo!"

Edward met us at the wharf. The British were patrolling the coast from Savannah to New York looking for smugglers. There was no time to be lost. The patrols had just passed on their northward leg of their patrol, so we must sail before they returned.

Edward gave me the latest news of the war. Washington had ordered a fighting retreat from New York, but Fort Washington on Manhattan Island had left it too late for their retreat and had been overrun. The Continental army had lost one hundred precious cannon, over one thousand muskets, and suffered three thousand casualties! The army had barely evaded General Howe as they retreated into Delaware. Had he not stopped to count his plunder and rest his men, he would likely have destroyed Washington's escaping army.

Brian Clancy showed me the official manifest. It showed all the appropriate duties had been paid and the cargo was heading for Bristol. Once in the English Channel, they would make a run for Brest to sell the precious cargo to the French and Belgian buyers at a much better price. *Banshee* had been modified a bit to accommodate her changing role. Her six pounders had been replaced with ten nine pounders. They had considerably longer range and a much bigger bite. She could still out run almost any frigate in the British fleet, and the larger guns could handle the smaller craft.

She sailed with the morning tide, and we headed back up river. We signaled to my sons on Beaver Creek, and Mr. Jones at Turner's Landing. We got the "all clear" sign at both places. However, when we arrived at Cheraw Landing, Mr. Llewellyn had an urgent message for us from Red Hat. His scouts had spotted a mixed war band of Cherokee and Creek, including the feared Red Stick band. They were sworn enemies of all whites and those Indians who helped them. They had determined it was a large band, but had not been able to get a better estimate yet. They were still just inside North Carolina, but some of the enemy scouts had already been seen in Red Hat's territory. He had sent word for the militia to assemble at Turner's Crossing. We rode hard for home. When we got there, our company and the other three were already assembling. Red Hat had devised a plan to intercept them.

There was an isolated Cheraw farm near the northwest edge of Red Hat's territory. No one had lived there for some time, but there were still livestock grazing the pastures. He had sent three elderly braves to wait in the cabin with a smoky fire burning. The enemy scouts were sure to see and smell the smoke and investigate.

As predicted, the scouts found the cabin and livestock. The braves made a show of running away from the cabin when the scouts appeared. They had left a well-stocked smokehouse, including two kegs of whisky. They sent two scouts back to find the main body, while the others made themselves at home.

When the main war band arrived, we would be ready for

them. We quickly mobilized our forces, and very quietly moved into position. Our company took position on a ridge one hundred yards north of the homestead. We moved our howitzers into position, but kept them out of sight. The four horses were kept quiet and moved back from the ridge. The company was spread out just behind the ridge. Company A was hidden in the woods along the most likely approach route for the main war band. We counted on the likelihood that they would assume their scouts had missed nothing and would be less cautious, and anxious to join the party. Bright's Company would take up position hidden in the woods south of the pasture and homestead. Company C would hide west of the cabin to cut off their exit.

The returning enemy scouts lead the main body of about four hundred warriors out of the forest from the east directly into the meadow. They could see their friends already had tapped the whisky keg and started feasting on the meats from the smokehouse. With a wild whoop of joy, they ran headlong toward the cabin. It was hard to wait. We were afraid that we would be discovered before we were ready to close the trap. They sent a couple of braves to slaughter a fat calf. The shot to its head echoed through the woods, but was hardly noticed by their comrades who were rapidly becoming drunk. Red Hat had made sure the whisky kegs were very large. They built a huge fire, and after butchering the calf, hung the meat up over green limbs to roast it over the flames. The Creeks and Cherokee gambled and competed in games of bravado, as the whisky worked its amber magic. By late afternoon, they had begun to sample the meat. Soon they were full and sleepy. The time had come. I sent a Cheraw runner to Company A.

They advanced in skirmish formation out of the woods 150

yards east of the cabin. They advanced unnoticed until they were within 75 yards. The groggy Indians raised the alarm, and began to search for weapons which had been dropped. Company A moved into three ranks. The first rank unleashed a deadly volley from the first twenty men, finding several targets. The second rank fired before the Indians had returned a shot. Their volley was equally effective, but seemed to jolt the war band into action. Seeing that the opposing force was only about sixty men, the war band straggled to attack. The third rank fired, killing several of the advancing braves.

The infuriated and emboldened Indians hurtled headlong to attack Company A, which began an organized fighting retreat. As soon as they began their retreat, the entire war band that was sober enough to fight launched a vicious pursuit. This was the signal for Bright's Company to pour fifty aimed shots into their flanks. In the chaos, they didn't notice the casualties. The second 50 men fired as their counter parts reloaded. The war band hesitated and turned to attack Bright's men. Just as they turned, we opened fire from the ridge with the howitzers loaded with canister. Each of the four guns cut down more than a dozen men. Our company along the ridge opened a staggered volley fire, cutting down more of the confused braves. Company A halted their retreat, and resumed the three line volley fire, advancing slowly into the meadow. The braves began to fall back on the cabin. However, Company C had taken up sheltered firing points from around the cabin, smoke house and other outbuildings. The fire from them turned the Creeks and Cherokee back into the middle of the meadow. The howitzers were reloaded, and belched out death again. This was followed by more volley fire from the ridge. That sealed their decision, and they turned as a body to try to penetrate what appeared to be the weakest opponent. They stubbornly charged straight south into Bright's Company. They were reloaded and ready. As the war band came screaming toward Bright's men, the front rank of fifty fired, followed by the second rank. The aimed fire from sober marksmen dropped dozens of Indians. As they opened fire, Company A intensified the pressure from the east, as did Company C from the farm buildings. Our company fired one more murderous discharge from our howitzers. As soon as they fired, we came down from the ridge into the rear of the disoriented enemy. They were receiving fire from every direction. Hundreds lay dead, and scores more were wounded and out of action. The Cherokee threw down their weapons, but the Red Sticks fought violently. At this point, Red Hat's men left our ranks and entered into a vicious hand-to-hand fight. Our remaining men continued to close with the war band, taking shots where they could. Soon we were all forced to join the close fighting. Our pistols were deadly, and our cutlasses and tomahawks were effective. Soon, the last of the Red Sticks were struck down.

They had killed thirteen of our number, and wounded twenty-two. The few Cherokee survivors were taken into the woods by the Cheraw. They returned alone, and we asked no questions. We fixed litters to carry off the wounded and buried the dead there in the meadow. We left the enemy unburied for the coyotes and crows. None had escaped to bring reinforcements. We had been bloodied in battle, and emerged more confident. We gathered the usable weapons and spoils of war. We called the battle Cheraw Meadows.

14

IT WAS MARCH 16, 1777, but this spring we would not plant any tobacco for export, only a few rows for our own use. Export to Europe looked unlikely, and barreled tobacco had a limited storage life. Indigo, being a perennial, would be tended, harvested, processed and stored. We certainly didn't add any new acres of indigo. There was a need for masts and spars by the British, but we had no navy. Therefore, we would not send timber down river. The tobacco acres were sowed to oats, corn, wheat, potatoes and beans. These commodities could be very useful in supplying our own needs and those of the Continental army. The Cheraw Meadow's fight had affected us deeply. The enemy had penetrated to within striking distance of our homes, and likely would have wrecked havoc among us but not for Red Hat's scouts. All of my sons, including twelve year old Mark, had fought beside me. They had handled themselves well. But the carnage had touched them, and me, to the soul.

All our children had one shade or another of red hair, and blue, hazel or gray eyes. Thomas, the eldest was twenty-six. He and Rebecca had a son named James. Thomas was tall and strong, with a knack for farming and livestock. He loved to hear, or tell, a good story and was quick to laugh. My second son, James, was twenty-four, and tall like Thomas. He worked hard on the farm, but his talent was with numbers. He worked with Mark Cunningham on our accounts. He was a bit quick-tempered, but not mean natured. Jane, twenty-one, was living with her husband on their plantation near Savannah. Aaron, nineteen, was still single. He was tall and broad-shouldered. He loved music and dancing. He was considered quite handsome by the young ladies. He was deadly with a rifle or pistol. John was seventeen, tall and thin. Like Thomas, he was a son of the soil. He understood the way of growing things, both plants and animals. Moses was fifteen, not as tall yet as his brothers, but stouter built. He was serious, thinking things through. He was stubborn like all of the Turners, but perhaps more than the rest of us. Mark would be thirteen in the summer. He was only 5'4" and skinny as a rail, kind and generous, with a heart for helping others. Being the youngest son, he had learned to take care of himself as self-defense from his big brothers. But because of his personality, all his siblings loved him. Mary was not quite eleven. She looked, spoke and moved like Priscella. She was a joy to all of us. Even if her brothers sometimes picked on her, they were intensely protective of her.

Priscella and I had fallen into the habit of lingering on the porch a while after lunch just to talk and share our thoughts. The view from the porch looked over the fields and the thick forest beyond. The front porch looked out across Turner's Crossing, with a prime view of travelers on the road. We had been married twenty-eight years and were still deeply in love.

On an evening such as this, she revealed to me how frightened she had been for the boys and me when we had gone off the fight the Creeks. What would become of her if the boys and I had been killed? I had never thought of it from her perspective. It made my stomach churn to realize the price even Priscella was paying for our freedom.

After Cheraw Meadows I felt more acutely the danger that now threatened our lives and livelihood. I had bought all the boys double-barreled Manton rifles like mine to give them an edge in a fight. When the Red Sticks had attacked, I had almost lost Mark. He had fired first one barrel, then the other, taking down a Red Stick with each shot. But before he could reach his pistols, a Red Stick with an empty musket swung it like a club at Mark's head. He screamed and rolled to the side just as Aaron stuck the barrel of his pistol in the attacker's ribs and killed him where he stood. Mark had been deeply shaken. Neither he, nor Aaron, mentioned it at home.

News reached us that Washington had moved his 2,400 men across the ice-choked Delaware River on Christmas Eve. They had marched all night along frozen roads to surprise the enemy in Trenton, New Jersey on Christmas morning. As the British Regulars and Hessian mercenaries were recovering from a night of feasting and drinking, Washington moved his troops into position. He took them by complete surprise. Of the enemy force of 1,500, over 1,000 had been captured. The rest had been killed, wounded or scattered. His army had captured badly needed stores of blankets, food, muskets and powder. He had pushed on to Princeton, New Jersey, where he inflicted another stinging defeat on the British. We had all been ready to hear some good news!

Some of the larger planters along the coast and the lower Pee Dee had close ties with England and were fiercely loyal to King George. They were called Tories after the English political party that traditionally supported the king. Here, we usually referred to them as Loyalists. Those of us who supported freedom from England were called Whigs, after the opposition party in England, although we had little support or sympathy from them. We referred to ourselves as patriots, although the name "rebel" was used widely by our opponents, and sometimes by us, too. We tended to be more from humble backgrounds, and more likely to be "dissenters" religiously. However, some of our greatest patriots, like Washington, were wealthy Anglicans. At this point, there was little room left for neutrality.

In July, we saw a smoke signal coming from Beaver Creek. We immediately began to assemble our company and sent word to the other three companies. Soon, another signal was seen from Turner's Landing. My sons Aaron and Moses came galloping to Turner's Crossing after lighting the signal fire. Four armed scows carrying saddle horses and Loyalist militia were heading up the Pee Dee. They were making a slow time of it as they were heavily loaded and the wind was contrary to use their lug sail. The scows flew a British ensign.

We had arrived at Cheraw Landing just ahead of the Loyalists. We had time to deploy the howitzers where they could sweep the landing from our hidden position. Some of the company had been unable to get there, but most had arrived in time. We had eighty armed deadly earnest men who did not intend to allow a Loyalist cavalry patrol loose in Marlboro County. The other companies had been alerted. They would arrive as soon as they could.

The scows nosed into the bank across the river on the Cheraw side. As they unloaded and started up the steep hill to Cheraw, musket fire from the Cheraw militia erupted from the woods along the road. The Tories dismounted and formed into line. They met more musket fire as they moved into formation. On the order of their officer, a body of approximately 120 men advanced into the woods. They were obviously well trained. The skirmishers in the woods disappeared before them. As the Tories advanced, they met heavy resistance from behind timber barricades. They had been drawn into a trap. The militia kept the Tories engaged long enough for most of Cheraw to evacuate. A church bell rang from the bell tower in Cheraw signaling that the town had escaped.

Hearing the signal, the militia made an orderly retreat deep into the woods, leaving skirmishers behind to discourage pursuit. The Loyalists regrouped and reassembled on the road where they remounted their horses. They rode up the steep hill into Cheraw, finding it pretty much abandoned except for a few Loyalist families. The District Clerk's office had taken their precious records with them. The Bank of Cheraw had taken their assets with them into hiding.

The hotel was ready and open for business, welcoming the invaders rather than risking the destruction of the hotel. The Loyalists did not realize that the inn keeper and his staff hated them, and reported their every word to the patriot forces. Not a few bowls of soup contained disgusting contamination.

Most of the mounted men returned to the scows and reloaded their horses and men. They rowed straight across for the landing. We waited impatiently for them to debark on our side of the river. Sweat poured off of me, and my throat was tight with anticipation. At my command, all four howitzers fired their deadly loads of canister. As the smoke cleared, our riflemen opened a murderous fire from behind covered positions. The howitzers fired a second volley, cutting down men like a sickle mows down hay. The few Tories left alive threw down their weapons and surrendered. Dead and wounded men and horses littered the blood-soaked ground. Wounded men groaned in agony, and the injured horses screamed in fear and pain. We ministered to the wounded men as best we could, and shot the suffering horses. Those horses that were uninjured were caught for our own use. The surviving Loyalists were brought inside the ferryman's inn where we had conveniently left Mr. Llewellyn and his sons tied and gagged. We did not want the Loyalists to guess their true allegiance. The dozen or so uninjured survivors were bound hand and foot, and guarded by twenty good men. The rest of the company boarded the scows and rowed across to Cheraw. We were met on the road by forty patriot militiamen who guided us up the well-known hill into Cheraw. The British flags were gone. The rebels knew which homes and businesses had welcomed the Tories. The remaining Tories were already under guard along with the Loyalists. The inn keeper was included in this group for the sake of appearance. The Loyalist militia were tried as a group and found guilty of treason. They were loaded into one of the armed scows under heavy escort from the Cheraw militia and taken down river to Georgetown and transported to Charleston for deportation to British territory at a later date. The local Loyalists were also tried and convicted. They were given the opportunity to renounce their allegiance to King George and swear allegiance to the independence of South Carolina. Those who refused were sent down river with the others. We sent word back to the other assembling companies that we would not need them.

The citizens of Cheraw filtered back in from their hiding places in the forest. Once their militia was firmly in control, we returned to the landing. The survivors there had been added to the scow heading for Georgetown in chains. Another armed scow with my men gave close escort to the scow containing the prisoners to discourage any mischief. The wounded were loaded on this second scow. The other two scows were taken to Turner's Landing and anchored as far up the creek as they could navigate and were hidden. They might prove useful later. Mr. Llewellyn and his sons were released as soon as the Tories were out of sight, as was the inn keeper from Cheraw. Our deception had saved them from future recriminations. We hitched the guns to our horses and marched home, some of us riding our newly acquired mounts. We had not lost a man, but blood had once more stained the rich, red soil of Marlboro County.

15

JANUARY OF 1778 BEGAN
in relative peace in Marlboro County. The British
wrongly assessed the sentiment of South Carolina
based on their association with the Loyalists along
the coast. They assumed the back-water Whigs were
beaten and subdued. They could not have been
more wrong. But we enjoyed the respite to renew
our supplies and to regroup. We sent a steady flow
of supplies downstream to be trans-shipped up the
coast in small craft for the Continental army.

We received mixed news from Edward. In
September, 1777, British General Howe had captured
Philadelphia and was using it as his headquarters.
The Continental Congress had barely escaped
behind Washington's lines to relocate to York,
Pennsylvania.

In October, American General Horatio Gates
had defeated British General Burgoyne at the Battle

of Saratoga. Burgoyne had surrendered his entire force of 5,700 men. This represented a large percent of the total British forces in the colonies. It was the greatest American victory so far.

In November, the Congress completed the Articles of Confederation. They were circulating among the colonies for adoption by the various Assemblies.

In March 1778, Thomas, Jr. and Rebecca had their second child, Aaron. He was named for Thomas' younger brother. We quickly had adjusted to being grandparents. It was a feeling that was hard to put into words. It was a warm, joyous feeling, but there was something almost intangible about it. Perhaps it was a feeling of completeness, fulfillment and accomplishment to our lives.

"Priscella, do ye remember when we first came here, there was naught but forest. Now there are homes, farms, and people."

"Aye, Thomas, my love. It has changed so much. It is filled with the boys we watched grow into men, and now their families. It is filled with the homes of our own children and their own children. We have been very blessed."

We sat in happy silence looking across our fields and the forest beyond them from our back porch. It was a good life, and it was worth fighting to keep it.

Whenever Turner Shipping and Trade ships docked in Charleston or Georgetown, they left discreet amounts of military stores. It was hidden in crates of trade goods. They would bring a few crates of muskets and bayonets. There would be kegs of gunpowder for cannon and small arms marked "salt." There would be cases of ready-made cartridges for the muskets and shot for the cannon. When James or Edward had assembled enough, it would be shipped upstream to Turner's Landing and hidden. Other loads were hidden in coastal traders carrying mundane cargos and smuggled to supply the Continental army in the north.

The British had sent a force of 500 men of the British 71st Regiment of Infantry, plus a troop of dragoons to occupy Cheraw. Their orders were to control the southeast bank of the Pee Dee and prevent incursions of rebel forces. They did not perceive any military objectives or significant threats coming from the brooding forested wilderness across the river. We were content for them to believe that for now.

On July 10, 1778, France declared war on their long-standing English enemy. This would keep the British occupied elsewhere and provide the colonies with some much needed relief. French warships and privateers would make it easier to trade with France and Europe, as well as distract the British navy from the American coast.

In August, we sent two armed scows to Georgetown with indigo from the previous year's crop. We met our friends from the *Banshee* once again. All the barrels were marked for delivery to Bristol as indicated on the ship's manifest. But we had other plans. Once in the English Channel, *Banshee* would head for the nearest French or Dutch port to sell the indigo.

Mr. Clancy delivered two cases of top quality English rifled muskets and bayonets to us. He also had two kegs of gunpowder, two cases of four pound ball shot, two cases of canister for the howitzers and three cases of ready-made cartridges for the muskets. We concealed the military stores among cargo of sugar, salt, and tax-paid tea.

We put in at Turner's Landing and hauled our illegal

cargo up Phill's Creek. The legal cargo continued on to Cheraw Landing where our wagons and teams hauled them home. Mr. Llewellyn, the ferryman, dutifully noted the transport of properly documented and taxed goods.

We stored the martial goods at the back of the pig pens. Each keg and case was carefully triple wrapped in oiled canvas. The whole area was covered with clean straw.

The Indian troubles resumed along the frontier. They were supported, supplied and paid by the British and their Tory allies. Isolated farms and small villages were being burned to the ground and their inhabitants slaughtered. Our regiment was asked to send assistance. Each of the four companies were now at full-strength of roughly one hundred men each, divided into five platoons of twenty under a lieutenant and two sergeants. Each company would leave behind a platoon of trusted men to guard the home front, while the rest left with the regiment. Colonel Marion had sent orders to head west northwest to try to intercept the raiders.

All of my sons marched with us. Mark Cunningham was a captain, serving as the regimental adjutant. Sean Perkins was regimental lieutenant of artillery, which consisted of our four howitzers on special carriages to be pulled by one horse each. They could go almost anywhere a man could go. We were, in every sense, a band of brothers.

Isham Turner was lieutenant of the platoon remaining in Turner's Crossing. He and his platoon would not be afraid to fight if necessary. The women and older children had been taught to load and fire muskets. Signal fires would call support of the other platoons. Riders could recall us home, but not quickly. This thought was never far from my mind.

Priscella's dread returned. Would we return whole again? Was the single platoon left to protect them enough to stop a war band? The men rarely realized the anguish and hardship of the women during war.

We were soon in southern North Carolina, continuing our west northwest course. Red Hat's men were leading the way, with scouts far out on both flanks and ahead of the main force. The scouts from the left flank quickly reported seeing thick smoke. They had sent runners to report to Red Hat, and the rest of the scouts proceeded toward the smoke.

We tightened up our column, and increased our degree of caution as we changed the direction of our march to follow the scouts. Soon, runners reported that a small village was burning in the valley along the Broad River. There was a large body of Indians and a handful of Loyalists. They had made camp and showed no awareness of our presence.

We would double our scouts in that direction and quickly move to take the high ground above the village. The scouts had estimated better than 400 men and had seen no artillery. They were drunk and celebrating their victory.

I assembled the regiment's officers for a council of war. We had to discuss our options. It was too late to attack them that night, but we must decide how we would attack them in the morning.

"My friend and brother, Thomas, we share our children and grandchildren. May I speak my mind to you?"

"Aye, Red Hat. We all value your opinion."

"I think two things may happen in the morning when we attack. They will run or they will fight. If they run, we will not be able to make them fight, and they will escape across the river. If they fight, they will come directly against us. I propose we take two guns and two companies quietly along the north bank of the river behind them. We will leave two companies with two guns on this hillside under cover. The men on the hill will open fire with round shot from the two guns to draw their attention toward them. If they want to fight, they will charge the hill and we will fall upon their rear. If they flee, they will run straight into our trap, and the men on the hill will attack their rear."

It was dangerous to divide your force in the presence of an enemy of equal or superior size. The full body could overcome any one-half of our force. The river's curve to the west would hamper their escape in that direction, but they could attempt to retreat through the woods to the east. It was a gamble. If they were surprised, it might well succeed. If they had any forewarning of our presence, we could be in trouble. In the enemy's drunken state, our chances at surprise were better. Even if discovered, we could still put up a vicious fight and perhaps win without surprise, and certainly did not risk total defeat on our part. We decided it was the best plan to pursue.

We moved quickly into position. The two companies along the hillside were in position just before sundown. They very quietly moved fallen logs and rolled rocks into a breastwork along the edge of the forest looking across the meadow toward the smoking ruin of the village. They set the guns where they would have a full field of fire across the meadow.

There would be no fires that night. Jerky, parched corn and water would be that night's ration. Double sentries were posted and regularly relieved. The rest rolled in their wool blankets behind the breastworks and got what sleep they could.

The remains of burned cabins and barns flamed and

glowed in the night. The victors were celebrating. The smell of roasting meat filled the air and caused our stomachs to tighten and our mouths to water. Drunken whoops were heard, as well as random musket shots.

Our two companies moved under the cover of the forest until we reached the north bank of the Broad River. Here we quietly dropped below the lip of the river bank. The edge of the river was timbered thirty feet or so out from the rocky bank. We could move out of sight along the river's edge. We had left the two howitzer horses with the north companies, as we could risk no unexpected sound. The howitzers were man-handled into position in the timber above the river bank. The men assumed positions just below the river bank for the night, but would move into the timber before light. We were about 150 yards south of the enemy. We also set our sentries, and the men tried to get some sleep.

Deep in the night, our sentries alerted us that two men were dragging a woman towards the woods along the river. We had little doubt of their intentions. They entered the woods directly in front of Red Hat's men along our line. They threw her roughly to the ground. As soon as the woman was clear, a volley of arrows felled the two men without a sound. Two Cheraw quickly fell on the woman to keep her quiet. She was terrified and tried to get away. Once she was securely silenced, I approached her. I explained who we were and why we were here. She could see that we had killed her assailants.

"We are here to save you. Nod if you understand. Do not scream or speak, just nod." She nodded as she looked wildly around.

"I will not allow you to be hurt, but I must keep your

mouth covered as we move you below the river bank. You must be silent. Nod if you understand." She nodded again, perhaps with slightly less terror in her eyes. We gently moved her below the river bank to the level sand along the shore.

"I am Thomas Turner, major of the Marlboro County Regiment of South Carolina. We are your friends. If we uncover your mouth, will you only whisper to us? Nod if you understand." She relaxed a little more and nodded. I indicated for the man restraining her to remove his hand from here mouth, but not to turn her loose.

"Thomas, bring her a blanket, some water and food." She shivered in fear and exhaustion saying nothing, but made no move to fight or run away.

Thomas wrapped a wool blanket over her shoulders. James offered a tin cup of water which she greedily accepted, and rasped out, "More." He poured her a second, then a third cup. She drank them quickly. We offered her some jerky and parched corn. She ate like a starving wolf, mumbling a weak, "Thank you." Drawing the blanket tightly around her, she fell into an exhausted sleep. I had Mark and John sit next to her. I was afraid she might wake up and cry out. As rowdy as the enemy was in their drunken state, I doubted they would hear her from this distance, but we could not take the chance.

I remembered the gambling phrase of "laying it all on the line." I had a different perspective of that as I looked along the river bank and saw all of my sons there. Would any of them fall in the morning? Most of the friends I had in the world were there. Would any fail to return home? What had I gotten them into? My stomach churned. It was too late to second guess myself now. We must go forward and do the best we could do. Above all, I could not let them feel my fears. I had no such fears when we had faced the Barbary pirates, but I had nothing to lose then. Now I had everything to lose. But if I sat back and did nothing, we might well lose it all anyway. I would swallow my fears and take the fight to the enemy. I felt determination replacing fear. I felt a rising hatred for these who had endangered our lives and for what they had done to these settlers. It could have been my own farm in flames, my own family dead. I felt the wolf rising in my throat, making me impatient for the hours to pass before I could unleash my rising fury.

As the faintest grayness showed in the eastern sky, we moved our men into position above the river bank. The howitzers had been loaded with canister. The men had relieved themselves, and had a quick cold breakfast washed down with water.

As agreed, just as the first ray of sunlight could be seen over the tree tops, the northern two howitzers fired solid shot into the sleeping drunken enemy. We could see them staggering to their feet. The guns fired again. The Indians and the few Loyalists among them began to point to the north, as the guns fired a third volley. They fired a few random shots with their muskets in the direction of the cannon blasts, but they were out of musket range. In small groups, they started to move toward the river. As a fourth volley rang out, they began to run in confusion for the river, straight toward the waiting canister and 200 armed men.

As they started their rout to the south, the hillside companies appeared from behind their cover in two long ranks of one hundred men each. They began to march resolutely toward the smoldering campsite. This made the confusion among the enemy complete. In panic, they ran headlong for the river.

The men under my command were to hold their fire until

my signal. At fifty yards, I roared, "Fire!" Both howitzers belched out their deadly loads of canister, and one hundred rifles fired. As the smoke cleared, we saw that we had killed many of them, and the rest had stopped in confusion. Our second rank fired. Many more of them fell dead or wounded. Some started back to the north away from the angry river bank. The northern column, now only seventy-five yards away, opened a deadly fire from their front rank. As they fired, the rear rank advanced and knelt to deliver a second volley. Our howitzers fired again, taking out a dozen each. Our men fired again from the woods along the river, followed quickly by the second line.

Knowing what lay north of them, and the unknown enemy strength along the river, most chose to take their chances there. Many stood immobilized by fear only to be shot down for their indecision. The cannon fired their lethal charges, slaughtering the closely packed Indians. At this point, our men emerged from cover and unleashed a savage attack on the disorganized enemy. They fired their muskets at close range and then drew their pistols. The northern column was now among them, wrecking carnage among them. Some of the enemy fought bravely, but the pressure from both sides had reduced them to only three dozen or so survivors. They threw down their weapons and tried to surrender. Our men rapidly reloaded during the pause.

From behind us came a blood curdling scream. The escaped woman had grabbed a musket from a startled militiaman. She ran wildly into the Indians, screaming as she ran. She suddenly stopped only a few feet from the nearest Indian. She raised the musket and fired, killing him. As she fired, several of the Indians grabbed their discarded weapons. Before we could react, they raised their tomahawks and killed her. Our astonished men fell on them at once. There were no longer any prisoners.

We had lost two men in the northern group from random musket shots, and another three during the frenzied hand-to-hand conflict. All my sons had survived. Even Mark, only fourteen, was covered in blood that was not his own. In the village, we found dead men, women, and children. There were twenty-two dead villagers in all. We buried them near their smoldering homes. We buried the dead white men, whom we had assumed to be Loyalists and buried our own five men. Our troops gathered any usable weapons, powder horns, cartridges and other useful items. We caught a few horses that had belonged either to the raiders or the settlers to take with us. The other livestock would slow us down on our return, so we turned them loose to their own devices.

We made a short march away from the scene of the day's battle for warm fires and hot food. There were extra sentries posted and they were frequently relieved, as all the men were exhausted. They were physically exhausted from the long marching and hard fight, plus the toil of burying the dead. They were emotionally exhausted from the stress of the battle and from the carnage they had seen among the settlers. Seared into their memories was the image of the enraged woman being cut down with tomahawks. We would never forget the memories of that day, but we would almost never talk about them either.

My sons were all sleeping around the same fire, as had become their custom on this march. I walked among them, touching each one as they lay sleeping. I did not want to wake them. I was shaking, not from the chill in the air, but from emotion. As I gently touched Mark's shoulder, he turned to face me. He was quietly crying.

"Father? I feel horrible. I feel mixed up inside. Is it normal to feel this way?"

I raised him up to sitting, and eased myself down on the ground next to him. I pulled him to me, and he sobbed in the quietness of the night, beside the crackling fire.

"Yes, Mark. It is normal this way. I have felt the same way every time I have had to kill someone. It shows that we are still God's creatures, that it pains us to kill another, even if they are evil men. You fought well today."

"I was afraid."

"So was I, son. So was I."

I held him until he fell asleep, then rolled out my own bed among my precious sons. I thanked God for sparing our lives, and prayed fervently for peace to come soon.

Red Hat's scouts found no other war bands in the area, so we headed home. The threat to our homes, our peace, had passed once again. The event we called the Broad River fight stained the ground with blood and the stench of death hung over the quiet meadow.

16

AFTER THE BROAD RIVER fight, our appetite for war, if there ever had been one, had turned to nausea. While we had experienced the indirect effects of the war for some time, the Cheraw Meadows fight, and now this one, had brought it to our doorstep in an agonizing way. We talked little of it, other than my report to Colonel Marion. John and Mark both had nightmares for some time.

We now knew our regiment could fight as a unit and execute basic field maneuvers. We felt more cohesive and effective as a military unit. In this regard, we felt more secure.

We had heard that the war in the north was rapidly becoming a stalemate. The British adopted a change of strategy. Since they had made little headway in the north, they would secure a strong foothold in the south, and roll the rebellious colonies up like a rug from south to north. They began by taking

Savannah by massive force. While they employed ships to keep the seaward-facing forts occupied, they made landings along the coast to approach Savannah from its vulnerable landward side. On December 29, 1778, Savannah fell, quickly followed by the capture of Augusta, the Georgian capital. We knew they would next turn their attention to South Carolina.

We were able to transport and sell all our stockpiled and newly processed indigo in 1779. With the British moving steadily up the coast, we wanted to get it moved before they controlled this part of the coast. We stored even larger crops of fodder and grain. We wanted to set back all that we could use, plus even larger amounts if the war came closer. We sent a coastal trader full of barreled grain and $500 in silver to Washington's troops.

In late January, 1780, we received word that British General Clinton with an army of 8,000 troops had boarded transport ships, under heavy naval escort, from New York to reinforce their forces in the south. Things were going to get worse soon.

By April of 1780, Clinton had his troops and ships in place for a full-scale attack on Charleston. Unloading heavy infantry and artillery with siege guns up the coast, he was able to move them to attack Fort Moultrie from its lightly defended and fortified landward side. The venerable fort was severely damaged. British ships were able to sail past the crippled fort into Charleston harbor to begin a furious bombardment of the town. They had bomb ketches with them that carried heavy mortars that could lob huge exploding mortar shells anywhere they chose into the panicked city. Fort Moultrie fell on May 6. The fate of Charleston was sealed. Hoping that reinforcements would lift the siege, the commander failed to evacuate the city by the one route open to them for retreat. No reinforcements arrived. The escape route was closed. Charleston fell on May 12, 1780, with the loss of the entire garrison of 5,400 troops and irreplaceable supplies.

General Washington sent Horatio Gates, the "Hero of Saratoga," to take command of the remnants of the southern forces. Reinforcements marched south from Delaware, Maryland, Virginia, North Carolina, and northward from Georgia. Gate's army was only 3,000 strong, roughly half Continental troops and half various militias. Gates was determined to bring the war to the British. He summoned as many militia units as were available to join him for an assault on the garrison at Camden, South Carolina. He mustered 3,300 troops, about 900 of whom were untried militia, eight light cannon and a small detachment of cavalry.

Word had reached us too late to send the whole regiment. There was no way we could gather the whole regiment in time. Also, our absence would invite the invasion of the 500 troops stationed at Cheraw. All the boys resolved to join the fight. I asked John and Mark not to go. They reluctantly agreed with me. Mark, Sean and Logan also determined to go. Dylan and Zachary also joined them. Sensing my reluctance for them to go, Tom Red Hat volunteered to go, along with six of his best braves. The group of 34 gathered their weapons and supplies and headed for the fight as fast as they could go.

They rode to Turner's Landing and used one of the hidden armed scows to cross the river with their horses. Four extra Cheraw warriors went with them to return the scow to its hiding place. They would wait there until their return. They referred to themselves as the "Marlboro County Volunteer Company." They were clothed in their buckskins and wolf skin hats. My sons carried double-barreled Manton rifles, and the others carried two rifled muskets each. They also carried two pistols each, cartridges, jerky, parched corn, canteens of water and wool blankets.

They moved quietly and quickly down back trails to avoid British patrols until they reached Gates camp outside of Camden. They were welcomed, and assigned to the 2nd Brigade under General Gist on August 15.

In the pre-dawn darkness of August 16 near the Sutton Farm eight miles from Camden, a squadron of British Dragoons rode into the pickets on the left flank of infantry under Lieutenant. Colonel Porterfield. The dragoons, who had been as surprised as the Americans, were quickly repulsed. They reported a large body of American troops spread across the road, stretching across the narrow ridge of dry ground between the swamps on either side of the road. The troops at Camden were under the command of British General Cornwallis. He had 2,200 troops, a company of dragoons, some Loyalist militia, and eight light field cannon.

Cornwallis immediately ordered his troops into battle formation. General Gates realized that there was a major British force only 700 yards in front of his superior force. General Gist's brigade was assigned to the American right flank. They were to cover any approach along a muddy track that followed the creek bordering the battlefield. They were to prevent the British from turning the American right flank. The shifting of British troops into formation caused some of the North Carolina and Virginia militias in the center of the line to believe they were already under attack by a much larger force. By four thirty in the morning the graying skies revealed the opposing armies only 200 yards apart!

Cornwallis sent the 23rd and 33rd regiments forward, directly east of the road, with Lord Rankin's Volunteers of Ireland immediately west of the road. They pushed forward in perfect order, shoulder to shoulder. The first rays of daylight glinted off their bayonets as the British marched steadily forward. Once they were within one hundred yards, the effect of the massed muskets would be devastating, and very likely to be followed by a bayonet charge. The American militia did not, for the most part, have bayonets, or an effective means to defend against them. As the enemy approached ever nearer, first a few, then a flood of the militia fled the field without ever firing a shot. Porterfield's Corps and the Continental Light Infantry angled their lines to try to close the gaping hole in the American center to their right. The Maryland and Delaware militias moved to their left to try to join up with Porterfield's troops, but the gap was too large to close. They attempted to attack the Volunteers of Ireland in the flank as they entered the hole in the lines, but the seasoned Irishmen were having none of it. They swung to their left to turn with a fury on the Maryland and Delaware units, driving them back with musket fire and bayonets. They slaughtered the militiamen, and the remainder fled to the rear.

Porterfield's Corps and Light Infantry were hit with a shattering charge of Dragoons commanded by the widely hated Lieutenant Colonel Banastre Tarleton. They succeeded in collapsing the American east flank, leaving the entire army in a desperate flight from the pursuing dragoons and infantry. General Gist's troops still held the west flank of the field. Cornwallis seized the opportunity. He sent the North Carolina Loyalist militia up the muddy track to attack the end of the line, while the volunteers of Ireland and the Imperial Legion Infantry launched a frontal assault spanning the entire front of Gist's badly outnumbered force. Their only escape was a fighting retreat into the swamp behind them. They would push westward into the swamp as they reloaded on the move, then turn and fire from the cover of trees in the knee deep water to pick off any enemy that tried to follow. The swamp made it impossible to proceed in military order and gave the advantage to the fleeing Americans. The accurate fire of the retreating troops was discouraging enough that the victorious British soon gave up the chase. The survivors in the swamp continued westward, until they felt it was safe to begin to swing back to more familiar territory.

The defeat had been complete. Over 900 American troops lay dead. Over one hundred were captured, as were all eight precious cannon. The rest were wounded. Only one hundred of the force of 3,300 American soldiers escaped. All the Marlboro County group had escaped, except Logan and Sean Perkins, who died defending the muddy road, holding off the enemy long enough for the others to escape into the swamp. But their sons and friends would live to fight another day.

The beaten group of men made their way back to Turner's Landing and the waiting scow. Two horses would return home without riders. The war had again spilled the blood of our family and friends.

17

GENERAL WASHINGTON rushed men into the collapsing south. The "over mountain men" from Tennessee arrived as did other groups both small and large. Cornwallis was determined to penetrate the now weakened southern frontier and effect a great pincher movement with the large army that was coming overland from New York.

Cornwallis' army had occupied a flat-topped irregular shaped mountain known as King's Mountain near the border between North and South Carolina. Gate's scouts had found them and reported that few or no pickets were placed below the mountain. Gates was cautious. The Tennessee men were eager to fight. They had a great hatred for the British due to the constant depredation they had suffered by the British and their Indian allies. These men represented a large part of Gates' force, and their feelings could not be completely ignored. The Tennessee men decided they were going to attack in the morning, with or without Gates. He gave in and they formulated a plan of attack. The troops quietly assumed their attack positions around the base of the mountain during the night.

In many places, it was extremely difficult to ascend the mountain in the dark. But in other places, the men were able to work their way up the mountain until they were in sight of Cornwallis' camp.

At daylight, they launched an assault that caught the British completely by surprise. The screaming Americans appeared like phantoms from the trees ringing the mountain top. They attacked with such ferocity that the outer perimeter collapsed upon the main camp almost immediately. The main camp was in the open and under attack from all sides. The Americans were among them before they could mount an effective defense. Fierce hand-to-hand combat erupted in bloody violence. Cornwallis and a rear guard were able to fight their way off the mountain, barely escaping with their lives. The British suffered over 1,000 casualties and the loss of huge amounts of military stores. The Battle of King's Mountain was a complete success, and very welcome news, not only to those of us in Marlboro County, but to the whole country.

Within a week, Washington sent his second-in-command, General Nathanial Greene, to replace Gates. Greene brought with him a new strategy for defeating Cornwallis and winning the war. He would lead Cornwallis on a "merry chase" deeper and deeper into the Carolina wilderness, and farther and farther from his line of supply. Our friend and kinsman, Francis Marion, was given the job of disrupting Cornwallis' supply lines and harassing the rear guard of his army. Marion and his men became notorious for appearing from nowhere attacking his supply lines, killing his men, and stealing the supplies. By splitting his force, he appeared to be in more than one place at the same time. The Redcoats called him The Ghost and The Swamp Fox.

When the British pursued him, he would disappear into the swamps along the Lynches River. He had a camp hidden on Snow Island where the Lynches met the Pee Dee. The British would not follow him there. His men would slip up the Pee Dee to raid one place, then showing up on the Santee to attack Cornwallis rear guard.

Lieutenant Colonel Banastre Tarleton was given the job of hunting the Fox. He was given permission by General Cornwallis to use "whatever means necessary" to stop Colonel Marion's raids. Tarleton took his orders to heart, burning homes, farms, and plantations all along the Santee, including Marion's own plantation. Men, women, children and livestock were slaughtered if they were identified by Loyalists as being rebels. Marion increased the frequency and ferocity of his attacks, but was careful to avoid traps set by Tarleton. Events would soon allow Marion to settle the score.

General Greene had laid a trap of his own. He drew Cornwallis into battle at a place of Greene's choosing, a place known as Cowpens in South Carolina. Greene summoned all available militia units to join him there.

We marched with our four howitzers and all our men except the customary rear guard. We arrived at Cowpens January 15, 1781. The force assembled there was the largest American force ever assembled in South Carolina. Cowpens was a gently rolling pasture of a few hundred acres situated in a deep bend of the Broad River. The river formed our left, right and rear flank. It was too deep to cross here. There would be only one direction for the British to attack us. A burned out plantation house was situated in the middle of the back third of the pasture on a gentle rise.

Greene split his command into two groups. He would command the Continental soldiers, and General Daniel Morgan would command the militias. The volunteers did not always follow orders well from officers other than those they elected from their own ranks. But they had a deep respect for Morgan, as he was known as an honest, brave man who was a fierce frontier fighter. They would follow him into the gates of hell.

The troops were placed in three bodies, roughly 150 yards apart. The forward group was where we were placed under direct command of Colonel Francis Marion. Our orders sounded simple enough. We were to wait to fire until the British were in range of our rifled muskets, but just out of range of their smooth-bore muskets. We were to reload and fire a second volley, then make a great show of breaking and running for the security of the second line. The second line was to fire two volleys, then turn and run with us over the rise. There we were all to turn and attack the pursuing enemy stiffened by the waiting seasoned Continental soldiers.

Greene knew the river would prevent any flanking moves by the enemy, especially their hated dragoons. The most hated man in South Carolina was commanding those dragoons at Cowpens—Tarleton himself! The encircling river would have a steadying effect on the militias. There would be no retreat, no escape. A large troop of the best cavalry in the south was stationed in the rear to quickly close any gap, or turn a threat from the dragoons. The rise in the ground would conceal the size of the force waiting there and the presence of the several light cannon and howitzers loaded with canister.

Cornwallis was in command of the 71st Highland Regiment with "their squalling bagpipes." They were dressed in kilts, and were hard, seasoned troops. Also under his command was the Imperial Legion, consisting of both infantry and Tarleton's dragoons.

Cornwallis could not believe the "stupidity" of Greene placing his troops in a situation that gave all the advantages to the British. He felt he finally had them at bay. After a brief cannonade by his limited light artillery, he ordered his whole force forward, including his reserve troops. Tarleton was to provide cover in case any American cavalry appeared, or "whatever the situation dictated."

With the bagpipes wailing, drums rumbling, and weapons flashing, the entire British force moved forward in precise order. At 200 yards, our motley appearing militia fired a stinging volley into the tightly packed ranks. Several of the Scotsmen fell to the well-aimed rifle fire. They marched resolutely forward. The militia fired a second deadly volley at one hundred yards. This time, more kilted soldiers fell. The militia turned and fled to the safety of the second rank of volunteers.

Seeing the wretched militia fleeing in apparent panic, Cornwallis ordered his men forward at the double. The front rank of the militia fired a volley at 200 yards, then stepped behind the now reloaded men of the first group. They knelt and fired a lethal blast. They retreated behind the former front line. They now also knelt and fired again at about one hundred yards. At this, they all broke and ran for the protection of the ridge behind them.

The militias' rifle fire had left ragged holes in the advancing ranks. The enemy closed ranks and continued. Seeing the Americans fleeing a second time, and the river blocking their escape, Cornwallis had his bugler signal the charge. His men tired from the fast-paced advance, called upon their reserves of strength and charged the gentle slope rising before them.

As they did, Tarleton could not stand to be left out of the kill. He ordered his dragoons to charge over the ridge into the broken, demoralized men he expected to find. As he did, William Washington's American cavalry charged straight into the flank of the dragoons. The dragoons' charge was shattered at great cost to the British and deteriorated into a desperate mounted saber combat.

As the Highland and Legion infantry topped the ridge they found a level area massed with infantry and artillery. The canister of the Continental cannon roared out great swaths of carnage. The British troops were stunned. Now they met determined volley fire in three long ranks.

"Front rank, fire!"

"Rear rank, advance. Fire!"

"Next rank, advance. Fire!"

Over and over again, the rifles slaughtered the astonished British. Some returned fire. Some tried to advance in ragged groups, only to be destroyed by the devastating rifle fire. The Continentals fixed bayonets and charged into the disorganized mass of men, followed closely by screaming militiamen.

The British ranks collapsed and ran for their lives. The Americans gave orderly pursuit, stopping to unleash withering rifle fire into the panic-stricken men. The British officers, mounted on good horses, ordered their men to "retreat in fighting order." But even Cornwallis had been seen galloping headlong from the field of death. As the bayonets of the Continentals reached the desperately fleeing men, a generalized hand-to-hand conflict followed. As the militia reached the fight with their tomahawks and cutlasses, the British infantry were falling like ripe grain before a scythe. The remnants of the dragoons tried to flee. They were hit hard by the American cavalry. Tarleton fled the field leaving his tattered command behind.

The smoke cleared. The killing stopped. The Americans had twelve men killed, sixty wounded. The British had 841 killed, wounded or captured. The Americans captured two cannon, 800 rifles, one hundred horses, and thirty-five wagons loaded with precious supplies. Our regiment had none killed and six wounded, and none of those were serious. It had been an amazing victory.

We all assisted in cleaning up the battlefield. We buried our dead and helped the British prisoners bury their dead. We had no place or provision for prisoners. Each prisoner who gave his parole was released, but with a small angular slash on their left cheek to identify them. If they ever raised arms again against us, they would be given no quarter. We took their boots from them, but allowed them to keep their canteens and some provisions. The British wounded were made as comfortable as possible, awaiting the return of their own army surgeons.

We did not linger on the battlefield but crossed the river at a ford a few miles down stream and set up camp in a good defensive position. All of my sons joined me around the fire that night. We set up a large officer's tent we had found in one of the captured wagons and slept there in relative comfort. I thanked

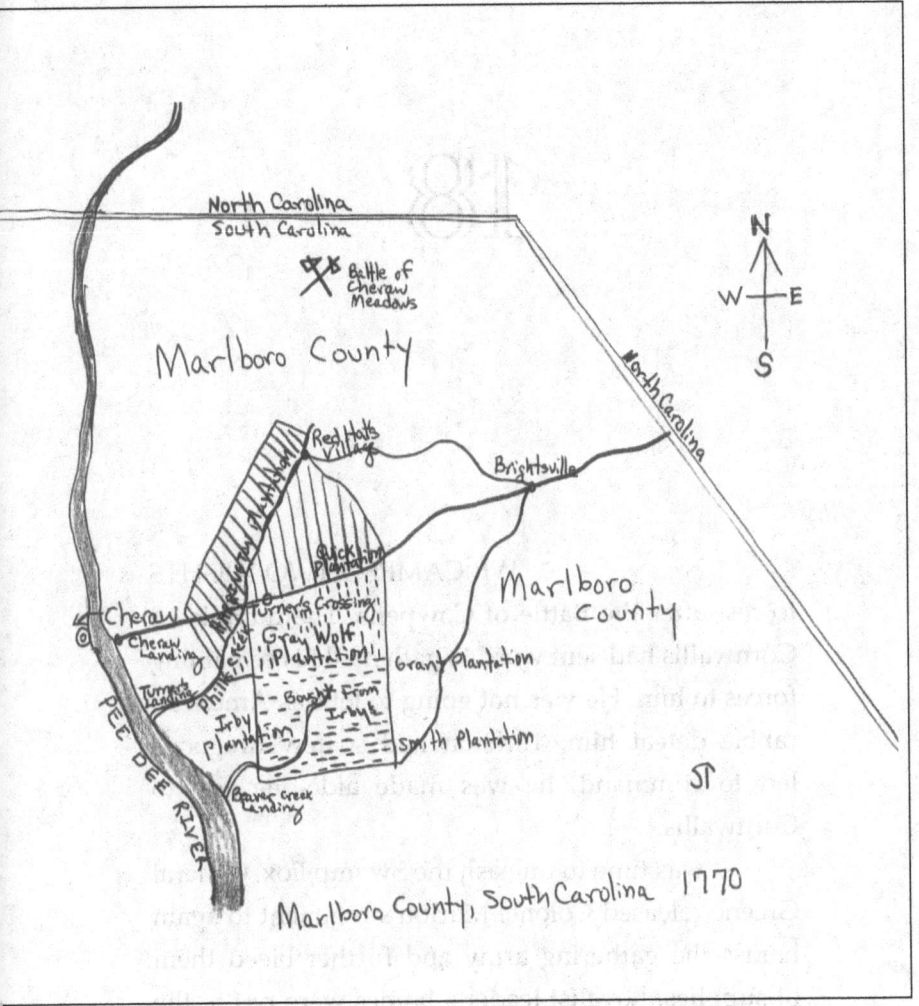

Marlboro County, South Carolina 1770

18

WE CAMPED TWO NIGHTS
to rest after the Battle of Cowpens. The humiliated
Cornwallis had sent word to gather all his remaining
forces to him. He was not going to let this American
rabble defeat him. Tarleton had so few dragoons
left to command, he was made aide-de-camp to
Cornwallis.

It was time to unleash the Swamp Fox. General
Greene released Colonel Marion's regiment to again
harass the gathering army and further bleed them
of supplies. Loyalist leader's homes were put to the
torch. British supply wagon trains would not move
without heavy military escort. Often, Marion would
decoy away the escorts with small parties, while the
main body rushed upon the supply train. Cornwallis
found concentrating and supplying his troops slow
and dangerous work. However, he was able for his

advance forces to maintain contact with the American force. Unknown to Cornwallis, this was exactly what Greene had wanted. The Americans continued a safe and orderly "retreat" northward. At each river crossing, we attacked the British, then fled. On each opportunity, a company would fall upon his rear guard troops and retreat. Red Hat's warriors would pick out the officers and kill them silently with their bows. The British were low on supplies, and their rations had been reduced. Each morning, a few pickets would be found with their throats slit, or pierced by an arrow. Their morale must have been low. Sometimes, they would turn and fire at shadows in the forest.

Knowing they were low on food, we bought an old dry milk cow from a farmer. We led the cow to a small pasture along a creek and placed a bell on the cow. Our main column moved steadily northward, but our company stayed back. We placed most of the company in hiding thirty yards from the cow in heavy brush. Red Hat's warriors were hidden in the forest on the other side of the road.

The hungry Redcoats marched by looking at the cow in spite of orders for "eyes front." Eventually, the lieutenant of the last platoon of the rear guard rode his horse out to inspect the cow, while his men followed on foot. They were hungry, and eagerly went toward the cow. They found her tied to a sapling in the meadow. Seeing the rope, they realized in horror they had fallen into a trap. At this point, our rifles spoke and every man in the platoon lay dead. With the first shot, Red Hat's men rained down a deadly shower of arrows on the remainder of the rear guard from their hiding place in the forest.

This caused a panic among the rear guard. They barreled up the road into the main column, as our men and Red Hat's braves slipped away. Dylan mounted the fallen lieutenant's horse and led the old cow back to our camp. We ate well that night.

On March 15, 1781, General Greene found the place where he was ready to give battle against Cornwallis' harassed and haggard troops near Guilford Courthouse, North Carolina. Our troops inflicted a terrible defeat on the British there. After the battle, Cornwallis headed what troops he had left northeast for Virginia as quickly as they could march. Greene would play cat and mouse with him all the way to Yorktown, Virginia, on Chesapeake Bay. But here, at Guilford Courthouse, he released the militia to return home with his thanks.

We arrived home on April 29, 1781. The regiment was dispersed and we set about our now late spring planting. Soon we were harvesting our wheat and oats. We had made arrangements with General Greene to ship supplies to him by coastal schooners to land at predetermined locations. Our surplus of cornmeal, flour, salt pork and jerky in great barrels, plus more barrels of oats for his horses were sent north along the coast. We were also able to send small kegs of powder and small arms with ready-made cartridges.

We mourned the loss of Sean and Logan Perkins. Their wives and families were devastated by their loss, as we were also.

There was a summer of relative peace in Marlboro County, while the rest of South Carolina chaffed under British control along the coast. We went about our routine activities for a change. We cleared forty acres of pine trees for pasture, stacking the timber along the creek to market when the war was ended. As fall came, we harvested our corn and stored it. We harvested our indigo and processed it. However, we put the barrels in storage until it would be safer to ship overseas. We had planted only enough tobacco for local use, sowing clover on those acres for grazing and hay to rest the land. There was no export market for the tobacco.

In November, one of the company scows came up river with a double crew of oarsmen. My brother, Edward, had rented Mr. Llewellyn's fastest horses to ride to Turner's Crossing. He had news.

In August, Cornwallis had gone to ground at Yorktown and fortified himself against the Chesapeake to await relief from the British navy. He expected heavy reinforcements from General Clinton in New York to be transported by a great fleet of warships. General Greene called up the area militias to strengthen his Continental forces and set siege to Cornwallis at Yorktown.

On learning of the situation and the opportunity it presented, Washington gathered his forces for a forced march to Yorktown, bringing more militias with him. He would not come alone. He was accompanied by the French General Rochambeau and a large army of French soldiers. French Admiral Count de Grasse set sail for the Chesapeake with a fleet of twenty-nine ships carrying an additional 3,000 soldiers.

The French fleet arrived at the mouth of the Chesapeake August 30. Two days later, Washington and Rochambeau's armies arrived overland. The British fleet arrived to find the French already in possession of the entrance to the bay. In a sea battle lasting from September 5th to the 9th, the French navy fought against the British fleet commanded by Admiral Thomas Graves. The French decisively defeated the British navy. The surviving British ships were forced to flee up the Chesapeake where they were effectively trapped by the French.

By September 28, 1781, Washington commanded a combined American and French force of 17,000 men, not even counting the troops on the French warships! Cornwallis' reinforcements had been aboard the defeated British fleet. He had a total force of only 9,000 men. Short on supplies and ammunition, and expecting no relief, on October 19, Cornwallis had surrendered!

I was dumbstruck with joy. Finding my wits, I sent my son, Mark, to ring the church bell. As soon as people gathered, Edward repeated the wonderful news. Riders left to spread the word to outlying plantations. We held a great feast in honor of the news.

In January, 1782, the British began to withdraw their troops from North Carolina. In May, we learned the British House of Commons had voted to end the war. The Dutch and French both recognized our independence. On June 11, the British had finally evacuated Charleston, and began to evacuate the garrisons at Cheraw, Camden, and Columbia. Finally, the British were gone. Many Loyalist families chose to leave rather than swear allegiance to our independent nation. Many relocated to Canada and the Caribbean.

In February, 1783, Spain, Sweden, Denmark and Russia recognized our independence. In Paris, the British officially ended hostilities on February 4, 1783, with the Treaty of Paris. Congress ratified the treaty in April, 1783. The last details were worked out about boundaries and legal details by September. The war was finally, completely ended.

Thirty-four years had passed since our arrival in the wilderness in 1749. There had been so many years, so many memories. There had been so much success and happiness, tempered with tragedy and sorrow. We carved an existence out of the forest of South Carolina and found so much more than we expected. We found peace, prosperity and freedom. But it had come at a great price. We paid with eight years of war, turmoil, hardship and bloodshed. But in the end, we managed to hold on to what we had made for ourselves with God's help and blessing.

Turner Shipping and Trade had survived, and had offices in Europe, the Caribbean, England, and all along the coast of the new United States. Our timber, mast and spar yard in Georgetown was thriving. The company banks had struggled and survived. The plantation was now my own. It had grown from raw forest into beautiful farmland, pastures and thousands of acres of still undeveloped forest. Our village had become a town of 150 people. It was a thriving center of trade and enterprise.

My family had grown. I was single the first time I rode the boundaries of the original acreage. Now thirty-four years later, I had a wife, six sons and two daughters. All of them were married now, and I had several grandchildren. The large cabin which had always echoed with many voices was quiet now. But Priscella and I were quite happy and still very much in love. Several of the children lived close to us, so we saw them almost every day. We saw all of the grandchildren often, except Jane's children in Georgia.

Most of our "band of brothers" who had come with us to carve out their lives from the wilderness were still near to us. All three Perkins brothers had died, but Sean and Logan had left children behind who lived among us. Our friend, Tom Red Hat, had grown old, but was still a strong and wise leader of the Cheraw people. Mark Cunningham was now a grandfather and a member of the South Carolina State Assembly.

Keenan had a sawmill of his own, a shop which built wagons, and a cooperage. He had more people working for him than I could count. His wife, Constance, had inherited the Grant plantation where they lived. Keenan was a grandfather.

Zachary Hawkins, once a cook's mate, was now a husband, father, grandfather and successful landowner. His friend, Dylan Caswell, former ship's boy, was also a husband, father, grandfather and farmer. He had some of the finest livestock in all of the Carolinas. He and Zachary remained close friends.

The wear and tear of endless voyages, storms, and the ravages of time had seen the good ship *Banshee* salvaged for scrap. Of her crew, only John Cook remained alive. He was an old man in Kingston, Jamaica.

Our plantations, Gray Wolf, Quick, and Harrington, still produced fine, profitable crops of indigo, tobacco, corn, wheat and oats. We grew almost all of our foodstuffs except salt, sugar, coffee, tea, and spices. Our grain mill was still very successful. I supervised the work of the plantations by horseback, but did little hard labor. I still enjoyed hunting in the fall with my sons, grandsons, and friends. Priscella kept a beautiful garden, but she didn't do all the work by herself. She cooked and kept house for me, which was enough work for anyone.

I came to realize I treasured our lives together as a couple, as parents, as self-supporting free individuals much more now that I had seen it all threatened, defended and reaffirmed. Not that I did before, but now I could never take any of it for granted. With God's grace, all that with which we had been blessed had come out of the wilderness. It was a wilderness no more. It was our promised land, our paradise, our home.

Epilogue

THOMAS TURNER DIED in 1794 in South Carolina. Thomas, Jr. died in 1822 in South Carolina. His son, Aaron Turner, sold his land in Marlboro County to a Samuel Hoodarm in 1821, and moved to Georgia. On May 12, 1828, he married a widow, Nancy King, in Georgia. It appears she had children from her first marriage. They then moved to Texas. The date is not well-established, but it appears to be prior to 1836. Aaron Turner died December 18, 1851, in Leon County. He left behind several children with Nancy, including Aaron Lloyd Turner (sometimes spelled Aron Loyd). Aaron Lloyd was born in December 17, 1850. Aaron Lloyd was my great-grandfather. The Turners moved further west to Callahan County. While living there, my grandfather, John Karr Turner, was born in 1890. The Turners migrated to the western edge of Texas in the early years of the new century, settling in Yoakum, Terry, and Gaines counties. My father, Aaron Lynn Turner, was born in Gaines County in 1931. I was born in Fayetteville, Arkansas in 1957. I was the seventh generation of my mother's family to have called the Ozarks home. We moved to Texas in 1966. My wife, Roberta, and I live in Plainview, Hale County, Texas where we have raised our daughter, Melissa Turner DeBusk, and our son, Aaron Lyles Turner. Aaron and Melissa are the eighth generation in lineal descent from Thomas Turner.

Genealogy

Thomas Turner, born Ireland = Priscella Alexander, born Ireland. Died south Carolina, 1794 or 1796 (records conflict)

Thomas Turner, Jr. born South Carolina = Rebekah (also recorded Rebecca) no last name found. Died South Carolina, 1822.

Aaron Turner, born SC =Nancy King. Died Texas, December 18, 1851.

Aaron Lloyd (Aron Loyd) Turner, born Texas, December 17, 1850 =Ella Fisher. Died Texas, February 22, 1939.

John Karr Turner, born Texas Decemer 12, 1890 =Effie Beatrice Smith. Died Texas, 1964.

Aaron Lynn Turner, born Texas May 2, 1931 = Doris Alene Combs (Alene).

Stephen Lynn Turner, born Arkansas January 10, 1957 =Roberta Ann Lyles.

Melissa Ruth Turner DeBusk, born Texas September 12, 1984.

Aaron Lyles Turner, born Texas January 19, 1988.

www.ingramcontent.com/pod-product-compliance
Lightning Source LLC
Chambersburg PA
CBHW011342010726
47493CB00009B/2925